CU00863973

Sin Bin 3

Tariq

Keith Miles

An Armada Original

Tariq was first published in Armada in 1989.

Armada is an imprint of the Children's Division,
part of the Collins Publishing Group,
8 Grafton Street, London W1X 3LA.

© 1989 Keith Miles

Printed in Great Britain by
William Collins Sons & Co. Ltd, Glasgow

Chapter One

On the first day of the summer term, the school was bathed in warm sunshine. Its main block – painted during the holidays – now looked almost welcoming. Its clean windows glistened with purpose. Its new perimeter railings added the final touch. The impossible had happened. Instead of the usual drab exterior, it actually had a surface brightness. There was even an atmosphere of hope.

Woodfield Comprehensive was at its best.

Tariq hated it.

Long before he got anywhere near it, he resented the school. It was inevitable. When he finally saw the place, it confirmed all his worst fears. In his view, it was ugly, noisy, violent. Woodfield offered no hope to him. All that he could sense was hostility.

Tariq Jahan was a tall, wiry Pakistani boy of fifteen. He had a thin, angular face with a suspicion of a moustache on his upper lip. Thick black hair curled down over his ears. Dark eyes smouldered as they got their first glimpse of the school.

It was a real dump.

Soraya took a kinder view. She was ready to give Woodfield the benefit of the doubt. Though she was a year older than her brother, she looked younger and more vulnerable. She had a quick, darting smile and a frail beauty. The family likeness to Tariq was quite striking.

The school did not seem too bad to her. It was smaller and older than the one they had just left but that might not be such a disadvantage. Woodfield certainly had a high proportion of Asian children. Soraya was pleased about that.

They went in through the main gates and strolled warily across the playground. It was already filling up. Some younger kids were charging wildly around, others were kicking a ball about, a few started an impromptu game of cricket. But most of the pupils stood in small groups and chatted. They complained bitterly because the Easter break was over yet they felt a grudging pleasure at being back.

Woodfield was home.

Tariq and Soraya found a quiet corner by the far wall. Both were nervous and apprehensive. While he continued to scowl darkly, however, she managed a brave smile. Soraya wanted to be accepted.

Like everyone else in the yard, they wore regulation school uniform but it did not help them to blend in. They stuck out a mile. Patently, they were outsiders. Untried newcomers who had not yet earned their right to be there. They aroused a lot of curiosity and some reflex enmity. Tariq stayed close to his sister.

But nobody approached them. There were glances and glares and sniggers but that was all. No one came to jeer or threaten. For the most part, Woodfield ignored them completely. That suited the two teenagers. They were left alone on the fringe of it all.

Their splendid isolation did not last. The door of the main block opened and a grey-haired man of middle years came strutting out. His back had a military straightness that made him seem taller than he was. Impeccably dressed in blazer and flannels, he had an air of elegant authority about him. He came to attention, produced a whistle and blew a shrill blast. It cut through the pandemonium like a knife.

The effect was immediate. Games were abandoned,

movement halted, conversations stopped in mid-sentence. Everyone looked at the teacher with mingled fear and respect. Nobody dared even to whisper. It was not worth the risk.

Soldier Stan was on duty.

Tariq and Soraya marvelled at the change. In a split second, the teacher had turned hundreds of children into standing statues. The silence was incredible. Soldier Stan, however, was not satisfied. His eye roamed the yard in search of a sacrificial victim.

'I'm *waiting*!' he growled.

They all froze on the spot. A deeper silence ensued.

Soraya was frankly terrified. Tariq remained watchful.

'That's better,' purred the teacher.

He kept them in suspense for a full minute then he blew his whistle for the second time. Woodfield responded to the signal at once. Quickly and quietly, the pupils lined up in order in serried ranks. Form monitors took up their positions beside each crocodile. There was a strong hint of the parade ground about it all. Everything was in its rightful place.

Except for the newcomers. Two forlorn figures stranded against the far wall. Lost, bewildered, embarrassed.

Soldier Stan snapped an order at them.

'Come over here! On the double!'

Tariq and Soraya obeyed the command. They walked past row after row of pupils until they reached the main block. The teacher brought them to a standstill with a flick of his finger then he regarded them with irritation.

'Who are you?' he demanded.

Soraya mumbled a reply that went unheard.

'Speak up!' urged the teacher. 'What are your names?'

The boy took a step forward and answered boldly.

'Tariq and Soraya Jahan, surruh. It's our furrust day.'

There was a momentary pause then Soldier Stan let out a rich chuckle. Seizing their cue, the ranks of pupils burst into laughter. What they had heard was so incongruous and unexpected. Out of the mouth of an olive-skinned Pakistani boy had come a broad Scots accent. It was hilarious.

Tariq bristled. He and his sister had only been there ten minutes and the whole school was mocking them.

Froggy Parsons used the edge of his gown to clean his horn-rimmed spectacles before putting them on again. He checked his appearance in the mirror, straightened his tie, breathed in deeply and drew himself up to his full height. A tap on the door interrupted the headmaster's preening.

'Come in!' he croaked.

His deputy swept into the study on high heels.

'Good morning, headmaster.'

'Good morning, Mrs Craig.'

'Another term begins.'

'Time will pass.'

He smiled at his own weak joke then turned to her.

Anthea Craig was a tall, big-boned woman in her fifties. She believed in wearing smart clothes with muted colours. She also believed in regular visits to the hairdresser. Her coiffure was always arresting. So was the aroma of her perfume. Froggy got his first whiff of it as soon as she came in.

'The school is looking nice,' she noted.

'Yes,' he agreed. 'Amazing what a lick of paint will do. Pity they're not going to spruce up the *inside* as well.'

'Any hopes in that direction?'

'None whatsoever, Mrs Craig.'

'Oh dear!'

'No money. They've spent all they're going to on us.

8

I'm afraid that Woodfield's now back at the end of the queue.'

'That's nothing new!' she sighed.

Froggy became conscious that she was towering over him. A short, squat man in a navy blue suit, he did not like to be reminded of his lack of height. Especially by female members of staff. He retreated behind his desk and felt taller at once. That was his power base. When he was at his desk, he soared above them all.

'What's on the agenda for today, headmaster?'

'First item is Mr Bowen.'

'Ah, yes.'

'Sad business.'

'We could be in for problems there,' she warned.

'Nothing we can't surmount.'

'Bryn Bowen is such a crucial figure in the school.'

'I'm aware of that, Mrs Craig.'

'Poor man!'

'A temporary setback, that's all,' he assured her.

A small pile of books lay in front of him. He gathered them up with a flourish and strode across the room.

'Time to make a start,' he announced.

His deputy stood beside the open door to let him pass.

'After you, headmaster.'

'Thank you, Mrs Craig.'

They came out of the study then walked side by side. His footsteps echoed along the corridor while her high heels provided a staccato accompaniment. They were an odd couple. Froggy marched along with self-importance. Mrs Craig trailed a cloud of perfume.

'I'll be saying a few words about the improvements,' he explained. 'We don't want graffiti all over the new paintwork.'

'Heaven forbid!'

9

'Oh, yes, and we have some new pupils joining us.'

'Two more Asians.'

'A school must reflect its catchment area.'

'Woodfield certainly does that!'

'Quite. Anyway, I'll be giving them a brief welcome. I want them to know what sort of place they have come to. In all the things that matter in education, this school is second to none.'

'Yes, headmaster,' she said tactfully.

They turned a corner and headed for the hall.

Harry Stanley loved authority. As he stood in the middle of the stage, he had the entire school under his control. The bulk of the pupils were seated in rows on the hard plastic seats. At the back of the hall – on wooden chairs that were a mark of status – was the sixth form. Members of staff occupied the more comfortable seating against the rear wall. When Harry Stanley was in charge, even his colleagues thought twice about speaking. He was such a strict disciplinarian. Under his gaze, you always felt on parade.

No wonder they called him Soldier Stan.

The hall was filled to capacity. Through the high windows along one wall, sunlight streamed in to give the place an ethereal glow and to equip dozens of undeserving young heads with a halo. In reality, as with all schools, there were more sinners than saints. Packed in together like sardines in a giant tin, the kids longed to stretch themselves and ease their cramped limbs. But nobody moved. Soldier Stan made sure of that. His ears were pricked for the first creak of a chair.

He barked a command that shattered the silence.

'Stand!'

As Froggy Parsons and Mrs Craig came in through the

rear door, the whole school rose to its feet. With his deputy at his heels, the headmaster went down the aisle and mounted the steps at the side of the stage. Soldier Stan waited long enough to collect a nod of gratitude from him then he slipped off into the wings.

A long table stood in the middle of the stage. Taking up his position behind it, Froggy slammed down the pile of books with a resounding thud. He had only brought them to make that one small dramatic effect. The head had many such tricks for gaining attention. Unfortunately for him, the pupils had seen them all. Several times.

'Good morning!' he challenged.

'Good mornin', sir,' droned the reluctant mass.

'Welcome back to Woodfield!'

There was a concerted murmur of protest and a few ironic cheers. Froggy Parsons was deeply unpopular. His nickname said it all. The kids found him small, ridiculous and slimy. Not surprisingly, he looked upon himself as a paragon. It never occurred to him that most of those who were now staring up at him were cursing him inwardly. He beamed back at them as if he had just been given a round of applause.

'I'm sure we've all got a productive and rewarding term ahead of us,' he continued. 'If we apply ourselves properly, that is. Let us begin by singing number one hundred and twenty in the school hymn book. "Blest are the Pure in Heart".' He signalled to the pianist at the side of the stage. 'Thank you, Mr Riddle.'

The music teacher attacked the keys to play the opening few bars. Ernie Riddle liked volume. He pounded the piano with all his might and braced himself for the moment when the singing started. It was truly dreadful. Flat, toneless and dispirited. The characteristic Woodfield sound.

11

Tariq stood in the middle of the row assigned to Form 4C. He was unable to join in because he had no book and because the words of a Christian hymn were meaningless to a Muslim like himself. All he could do was to glower at those around him. The place felt so alien to him. His resentment grew.

Soraya was six rows behind him with the pupils of 5B. The girl next to her shared her book so that they could both read the words of the hymn. Unlike her brother, Soraya did make an effort to take part. She mouthed the words soundlessly.

> 'Lord, we Thy Presence seek,
> May ours this blessing be;
> Give us a pure and lowly heart,
> A temple meet for Thee.'

Ernie Riddle brought the suffering to an end with some thunderous chords. Groaning with relief, the congregation sat down. When the noise subsided, Froggy assailed them with a long passage from *Readings for Morning Assembly*. It extolled the virtue of Obedience and he hammered the point home. A token prayer followed then the headmaster really came into his own.

As he warned them to respect the fabric of the school, he used his full repertoire. He pointed a menacing finger, punched the air with his fist, clapped his hands together, banged the table then stamped on the floor. It was typical Froggy stuff.

Tariq only half-listened. His mind drifted off to the school he had left behind in Glasgow. It had so many things that Woodfield did not have. More room. Better facilities. A warmer atmosphere. And friends. When he

12

thought about those friends, he was overwhelmed with a sense of loss. He might never see them again.

Froggy's voice jolted him out of his reverie.

'I want to give a special welcome to our new pupils, Tariq and Soraya Jahan. They come from Pakistan by way of Scotland.'

A ripple of amusement ran through the hall. The boy next to Tariq gave him a playful dig in the ribs. The girl on the other side of him just giggled uncontrollably. Tariq and Soraya were being mocked anew.

Froggy did another foot-stamp to quell the noise.

'And now I have some rather distressing news for you,' he said with measured solemnity. 'During the holidays, Mr Bowen was injured in a climbing accident. He will be away from school for some weeks.'

There was a mild riot of speculation. Basher Bowen was the massive Welshman who acted as Dean of Discipline. He seemed quite indestructible. Nobody could believe that he had really hurt himself. A wave of sympathy came. Basher was a genial martinet. The kids were at once wary and fond of him. He would be missed.

'Meanwhile,' resumed Froggy, 'there will be a change at the Annexe. Mr Bowen's duties will be taken over by Mr Stanley.'

This time the response had no affection in it. Soldier Stan was a different kettle of fish. They would love *him* to have a climbing accident.

Tariq could not understand what was going on. He did not realize the significance of the headmaster's announcement. It would colour the boy's first term at Woodfield. If Soldier Stan went to the Ainsley Annexe, it could mean only one thing.

The Sin Bin would become intolerable.

* * *

13

They went for him at the first opportunity. The school had plenty of Asian children with strong Midland accents but nobody found this unusual. A Scots Pakistani, however, was a novelty. They let Tariq know it.

'Where's your kilt, then?'

'Show us your sporran!'

'Can you play the bagpipes?'

'D'you know thar Billy Connolly, like?'

'Wass in your sannwich box, then – porridge?'

'Nah!' corrected another joker. 'Iss 'aggis!'

Laughter surrounded him like a swarm of bees.

The mid-morning break found Tariq in the playground with his classmates. They pursued him relentlessly until he swung round and yelled at them.

'Och! Away with you!'

But the sound of his voice only produced fresh bursts of merriment. They began to mimic him and urged him to speak again. He decided to hold his tongue and the tactic eventually worked. Tired of baiting him, the others wandered away. Tariq was able to seek out his sister to compare notes.

'It's terrible!' he complained.

'Only for a wee while.'

'4C must be the wurrust class in the school.'

'5B is OK,' said Soraya. 'I've made one friend already. Her name is Munni. She went to Pakistan in the holidays.'

'Wish *I* was there now!'

'It'll get better, Tariq.'

'Never!' he retorted, looking around in disgust. 'Woodfield is a prison.'

'Give it a chance.'

'I blame Father for this.'

'It's no his fault.'

'He brought us doon here, didn't he?'

'Only because he had to. Father explained that.'

'This place is hell.'

'Tariq . . .'

'I want to go back to Glasgow.'

'So do I,' she said wistfully. 'But we're stuck here. Why not try to make the most of it?'

'I'll no put up with this!' he vowed.

'What choice have we got?'

He was about to answer her when he became aware that they were being watched. Two boys were standing some ten metres away and sniggering at them. Both were from 5B. Pancho Reeves was a big, fleshy youth with close-cropped hair and piggy eyes. Mike O'Brien was short, dark and thickset. A broken nose set the tone for his face.

'What do those idiots want?' hissed Tariq.

'Let's move away,' suggested his sister.

'I'm no afraid of them.'

'Come on.'

She took him by the arm to lead him away but they only got a few steps. Their way was suddenly barred by the two boys. They leered at Soraya then turned on Tariq. Pancho curled a lip.

'You 'er brother?'

'No, I'm her great-grandfather,' came the sarcastic reply.

Mike O'Brien smirked but Pancho was not amused.

'Doan ger funny with me!' he cautioned.

'Then leave us alone,' said Tariq.

'We haven't done anything to you,' argued Soraya.

'An' *you* shut your cake-'ole an' all,' snarled Pancho. 'I'm talkin' to your little brother 'ere. Gorrit?'

'What do you want?' asked Tariq.

'To give you a friendly warnin', like.'

'Why?'

'Juss so you know 'ow things stand.'

15

'We're in 5B,' said Mike.

'We *are* 5B,' emphasized the other.

'Thass right. Panch an' me are the boss men, see.'

'We're in charge.'

'Of everythin'.'

'What's this got to do with me?' wondered Tariq.

'Look in a mirror,' advised Mike.

'Eh?'

'We doan like wogs,' explained Pancho with an oily grin. 'They stink the place out. Right, Mike?'

'Right, Panch.'

'But *I'm* in 5B,' admitted Soraya.

'Yeah,' replied Mike. 'We noticed the smell.'

'Don't speak to my sister like that!' said Tariq vehemently.

'Temper, temper!'

'Stop bothering us.'

'Iss *you* who's botherin's *us*,' growled Mike.

'Ger the message?' added Pancho. 'Wogs go 'ome!'

'We were born in Britain,' said Soraya.

'We have as much right to be here as you,' insisted Tariq.

'Nor while you're at Woodfield.' Pancho moved to within inches of the Pakistani boy. 'Keep out of our way. Unnerstand?'

'Or there'll be trouble,' warned Mike.

'Big trouble,' confirmed his friend, holding up a fist by way of advertisement. 'Ger the picture? Doan 'ang round 5B waitin' for your sister. Iss out of bounds to you. We gor enough of a pong in there as it is.'

He pushed Tariq in the chest and the boy stumbled back.

Pancho Reeves and Mike O'Brien strode away happily.

16

They liked frightening the Asian kids. They were good at it. After their little chat with Tariq, they were convinced that he would be no problem at all.

But they were quite wrong.

Chapter Two

Don Sheen poured tea into the two mugs then brought them across to the window. After setting them down on the low table, he flopped into his armchair and nodded towards the drinks.

'Yours is the one with the handle.'

'Thanks.'

'Milk in the carton.'

'So I see.'

'Help yourself to sugar.'

Harry Stanley eyed the open bag with distaste.

'I hadn't realized it was so primitive over here.'

'Oh, it's not too bad now,' said Don breezily. 'At least, they've stopped eating the missionaries.'

The older man shot him a look of disapproval before taking a small box from his pocket. He added two artificial sweeteners to his tea before stirring it with a bent spoon.

They were sitting in the back bedroom of the Edwardian town house that had become the Ainsley Annexe. It was here that the school troublemakers were sent for special treatment. On the first day of term, only a clutch of regulars were there. From their vantage point in the window, the teachers could look down on their charges who were taking their lunch break in the narrow confines of the yard at the rear of the house.

'I really pitched into them this morning,' said Soldier Stan.

'So I heard.'

'Start as you mean to go on. That's my motto.'

'But you won't be here indefinitely.'

'Long enough to make an impact.'

'I see.'

'The Sin Bin needs an injection of cold steel,' decided Soldier Stan. 'I think I'm the right man to provide it.'

Don Sheen made no comment. Along with Basher Bowen, he was a permanent feature at the Annexe. Notwithstanding their different approaches, the two men got on very well together and this made the administration of the place a lot easier. A radical change had now taken place. Soldier Stan had his own ideas.

'I'd like to close the Sin Bin down.'

'Who wouldn't?'

'Valuable property is going to waste here. It should be used for true educational purposes.'

'It is. We teach the drop-outs.'

'You incarcerate the school thugs, that's all.'

'There's more to it than that, Harry.'

'Not in my view. What we must do is this. Make the place so thoroughly unbearable that nobody will dare to be sent here. That way we clear everyone out and start afresh.'

'It works in theory but not in practice.'

'Just you watch! I'll empty the Annexe in a fortnight.'

Don Sheen winced. He was much younger, more relaxed and more idealistic than his colleague. They were worlds apart. While Soldier Stan believed that smartness was next to godliness, Don opted for denim trousers, an open-necked red shirt and a tired-looking leather jacket. He noted the way that the other man's black shoes gleamed. Don himself wore an old pair of trainers.

A clash between them was inevitable.

'The regime here is too soft,' alleged Soldier Stan.

'Try telling that to the kids.'

19

'You and Bryn should take a tougher line.'

'That's a matter of opinion, Harry.'

'Well, I'm giving you mine now,' said the other, getting into his stride. 'The army method is the only way. Stern discipline and regimentation. I've had first-hand experience of it and it always does the trick. They must be beaten into shape.'

'They're children – not recruits.'

'Comes to the same thing.'

'I don't go along with that.'

'Keep them to the whistle. That's the secret.'

'You sound like an animal trainer.'

'I am. This is Woodfield, remember.'

The cynicism of the remark was chilling. Don did not trust himself to reply. Harry Stanley was a type. Most schools seemed to have a version of him on their staff. He was well-qualified, conscientious and ready to speak his mind. He showed all his colleagues a kind of brisk politeness. Underneath the impressive exterior, however, was a rock-hard disciplinarian who hated kids.

In the large staff room at the main school, Don had never had to exchange more than a few words with him. Their relationship had been pleasant but distant. Now they were yoked together, forced to work in harness at the Ainsley Annexe. It would be hard going.

Soldier Stan leaned forward to rap on the window with his knuckles. The horseplay down in the yard ceased at once and the boys involved moved guiltily apart. The teacher sat back.

'See what I mean? Don't give them an inch.'

'They're kids, Harry. They must have some freedom.'

'Not while I'm around.'

'You have to strike a balance.'

'The only thing *I'll* strike is a few heads.'

Don Sheen gulped down his tea then got up to refill his mug. The omens were all bad. Soldier Stan was there to impose his personality on the place. Life in the little staff room lost all its appeal but there was an additional problem. Don had his own techniques of dealing with the pupils who were sent there. His work was going to be severely impeded.

'By the way,' said the older man, 'how *is* Bryn?'

'Slowly on the mend.'

'Which leg was it?'

'The left one. Double fracture.'

'Bad luck. Any idea when he'll be back?'

'Soon, I hope,' muttered Don to himself.

The sooner the better.

The Ace Garage occupied a corner site in the most run-down part of the district. Its six new pumps and its neon-lit canopy were in stark contrast to the dull, fatigued terrace housing all around. Next to the garage were three other small businesses – a pet shop, a butcher's and a video rental store. In each case, the owners lived above their premises.

Atlas Jahan did not own the Ace Garage. He was simply its manager. His name suggested a muscular man with excessive strength but he belied it. Now in his late thirties, he was scrawny, balding and of medium height. His wife, Hamida, was plump, docile and several years younger than him. While he wore a sweatshirt and jeans, she was in traditional Pakistani costume. Her long veil sat on the back of her head and set off a face that had been lean and lovely before she had three children. Motherhood had taken its toll.

They were in the small living room at the rear of the garage. Paintings of their native land, copper vases and an

Afghan carpet gave it an Asian feel. There were large cushions on the floor beside the sofa.

Their elder son, Mo, was looking after the cash desk. That gave Atlas the opportunity to study the account books. He went through the figures with a deep frown etched on his brow. Hamida sat at the table and prepared food for the evening meal. She knew better than to interrupt her husband. Every so often, she glanced up at the ornate clock on the wall.

Tariq and Soraya would be back any moment. Their father had not spared them a thought all day but they had never been out of their mother's mind. Going to a new school entailed all sorts of difficulties. She worried continuously about her children. Tariq could be too aggressive and Soraya was far too gentle. They could both suffer at a place like Woodfield.

Footsteps approached from outside then the door opened. She got up at once to welcome them back. Atlas was hardly aware of their presence.

They spoke in Urdu, their national language.

'How was it?' asked Hamida anxiously.

'Fine,' said Soraya.

'No, it wasn't,' claimed Tariq, dropping his bag to the floor.

'Why not?'

'The school is awful, mother!'

'Oh!'

'I just can't stand it there.'

'We've only been at Woodfield one day,' Soraya reminded him.

'One day too many,' said her brother ruefully.

'It will take time to settle in,' she urged.

'I *never* want to settle in there!'

22

The argument wrested Atlas away from his account books. He looked up irritably and clicked his tongue.

'What's all this noise? Can't you see I'm busy?'

'Sorry,' murmured Soraya.

'I must talk to you, Father,' asserted Tariq.

'Not now, boy.'

'But it's important.'

'So is running this garage. It's our livelihood.'

'I've been thinking about that.'

'Then let me get on with it.'

'No,' persisted Tariq, risking his father's anger. 'You must hear me. Please. This can't wait.'

Atlas glared at him then snapped one of the books shut.

'All right, Tariq,' he said quietly. 'What is so important that it can't wait? Tell me.'

The boy had worked out what he was going to say but the words would not come. He had great respect for his father and had never dared to question any of his decisions before. As doubts nudged him, he ran his tongue over his dry lips.

'Come on!' ordered Atlas. 'Spit it out, boy.'

Tariq threw caution to the winds and blurted it out.

'I'm going back to Glasgow, Father.'

'*What*?'

'To my old school.'

'Have you gone mad?'

'I know how we can do it,' gabbled Tariq. 'I can live with Uncle Roshan and help in the shop at the weekends. I'll earn my keep, I promise, and I'll do everything Uncle Roshan tells me. That way I can go back to my old school. The other thing is – '

'Shut up,' said Atlas.

'It will be one less mouth to feed here. In any case – '

'Shut up!'

'I've made up my mind so that's that.'

'SHUT UP!'

The yell was backed up with action. Leaping from his chair, Atlas slapped his son hard across the cheek. Hamida gasped, Soraya let out a whimper and Tariq fought off tears. The shock of it all hurt him as much as the pain. It was a long time since his father had struck him like that.

Atlas stared coldly at him and laid down the law.

'You are my son,' he said pointedly. 'And you do what *I* tell you. Nobody is going back to Glasgow. Our home is here now. You will stay here – and you will like it.'

He turned on his heel and went out swiftly.

Tariq felt wounded and betrayed.

His bid for freedom had failed.

Graham Reeves lay on his back beneath the car and made some final adjustments with a spanner. The tool slipped and fell to the ground with a clatter. Swearing loudly, he groped around for it. When he found it again, he applied it once more to make one last twist. The job was done.

'Pancho!' he called.

'Yeah?'

'Pass me thar torch.'

'Why?'

'Why'd you think, numbskull? So's I can bloody well *see*!'

'Oh, yeah.'

'Gerra move on, then.'

'Grab 'old,' said his younger brother, handing him the torch. 'Like me to start 'er up, Gray?'

'Nor while I'm under 'ere, you idiot!'

'Keep your 'air on.'

'Then talk sense. If thass possible.'

Graham Reeves used the torch to inspect what he had

24

done. It was an old Vauxhall Cavalier with rusting body-work and fading colour but it was all he could afford. To lessen his running costs, he looked after the maintenance himself. That meant that he was almost always out in the street fiddling with the vehicle.

As he rolled out from under the car, a dog trotted up and tried to lift its rear leg against the wheel. The proud owner gave such a howl of righteous indignation that the animal scampered off as if it were in the greyhound Derby.

'Thass *all* I need! Dog pee on my 'ub-caps!'

'Coulda been worse,' his brother pointed out.

'Very funny!'

'Thought you'd like it.'

'Do something useful, our kid. Pull us up.'

'OK.'

Pancho took his brother's hand and heaved hard. Graham was back on his feet in an instant. Pancho immediately regretted his good deed.

'My 'and's covered in oil!'

'Thass odd,' joked Graham. 'So's mine.'

'You mighta warned me.'

'Wipe it orff on your 'ead. Nobody'll notice the diff'rence.'

'Thanks a bunch!'

Graham pulled a rag from the pocket of his overalls and used it to wipe his own hands. Then he tossed it to his brother.

'Ta.'

'No charge.'

'Can I start the car up now?'

'You 'avenn gorra licence.'

'Aw, come on, Gray. You said I could!'

'Later, maybe.'

'*Now*!'

'I'll think abourrit.'

Pancho Reeves might be one of the self-appointed boss men of 5B but he had to play second fiddle at home. His brother was a burly character of nineteen with shoulder-length hair that was held in place by a spotted bandana. With his face grimed with dirt and oil, he looked like an Apache Indian.

Graham was another product of Woodfield. He had been a real tearaway in his time and had paid several visits to the Sin Bin. He looked back on his old school with cheerful disgust. Graham had a part-time job in a city centre pub. It kept him busy on most evenings but it did not pay too well. He therefore had to find a way to supplement his income.

'Tell us about Sunday,' said Pancho eagerly.

'Iss the day arfter Sat'day, innit?'

'You know wor I mean! Sunday night.'

'Oh . . . thar.'

'Who was 'e?'

'Dunno. Some stupid Paki, thass all.'

'Where d'you gerrim?'

'Mind your own business.'

'An' 'ow much did 'e 'ave on 'im?'

'Coupla 'undred.'

'Gray! Thass fantastic!'

'Nor really,' said his brother airily. 'There was three of us. Finished up with seventy quid each.'

'For five minutes of Paki-bashin'.'

'Thass the goin' rate, our kid.'

'Yeah!'

Pancho's piggy eyes glowed. Like him, Graham had started by bullying the Asian children at Woodfield. He had now graduated to demanding money with menaces and to common assault. Pancho envied him and the apparent glamour of his lifestyle.

'Lemme come with you one time.'

'No!'

'*Please*. I woan ger in the way.'

'You're always in the flippin' way.'

'Juss take me along.'

'Forgerrit, Pancho.'

'I wanna see 'ow you do it.'

'Find your own Paki to bash.'

Graham grabbed the oil-stained rag from his brother and went off into the house. Pancho was crestfallen. Then he heard the last sentence again.

'Find your own Paki to bash.'

A dark smile spread slowly across his face.

Calvin Hubberd was a short, stubby Jamaican boy with a centre parting. A missing front tooth turned a dazzling grin into something more sinister. Calvin's problem was that he kept getting into trouble. In his blithe way, he put it down to bad luck. There was no real harm in the boy. Just a lot of mischief that bubbled over.

On the second day of the new term, he fell from grace once more. Froggy Parsons gave him the usual lecture then imposed the maximum sentence. A trip to the Ainsley Annexe.

Soldier Stan answered the door to the newcomer.

'What do *you* want, Calvin?'

'Please, sir. Mr Parsons sent me, sir.'

'Why?'

'I'm to give you this, sir.'

Calvin handed over the envelope which had been pressed on him by the headmaster. Soldier Stan extracted the letter and read it with interest. He looked back at the boy. Calvin tried to win sympathy by flashing his gap-toothed grin but the teacher was impervious to it. He put a hand around the boy's neck.

'Step inside, sonny!'

Calvin was yanked into the hallway without ceremony and the door was closed behind him. Things had altered. Last time he was there, he had been ribbed by Basher then taken into the main classroom. Soldier Stan was offering a harder road.

'So? You've been making a mess in the art room.'

'Nor really, sir.'

'You threw paint on the floor.'

'No, sir. Honess, sir.'

'Don't lie, Calvin Hubberd.'

'I'm nor lying'.'

'And don't argue with me.'

'I'm nor arguin'.' The boy cowered as a hand was raised in threat. When it was withdrawn, he continued his defence in a whisper. 'It was an accident, sir.'

'Ah. You did do it but you didn't mean to.'

'Yeah. Thass right.'

'Your whole life is one long series of accidents, isn't it?' sneered the teacher. 'You're nothing but a pain in the backside to all of us. It's got to stop.'

'Yeah, sir.'

'Once and for all. We'll have to teach you a few lessons.' Soldier Stan thought for a moment then smirked. 'The first thing you must learn is how to keep floors clean. Because when you make a mess, Calvin Hubberd, somebody has to mop it up. Wait here!'

The boy did not budge an inch. He was frightened.

Soldier Stan went down the corridor and in through a door. The living room of the house now did duty as a classroom and half a dozen boys pored over their desks.

Ground down by the new order, none of them even dared to lift his eyes from his work. The teacher opened the drawer in the table, took something out then went back into the corridor.

'Come to me, Calvin.'

'Yeah, sir,' he said, trotting over.

Soldier Stan held a box in the palm of his hand.

'Do you know what this is?'

'Iss a box, sir.'

'No, boy. It's a box of paper clips.' He shook them till they rattled. 'Can you guess how many are in here?'

'Er . . . not really, sir.'

'Then you'd better count them.' He opened the box and scattered its contents along the corridor. 'Get weaving!'

Calvin gulped. 'All of them, sir?'

'Down on your hands and knees!'

'Yeah, sir,' said the boy, obeying at once.

'Now clear up this mess from the floor.'

He went back into the classroom but left the door ajar. The Jamaican reached for the box which had been discarded along with the paper clips. He read the sticker on the cover. The box contained five hundred clips. He blenched. Even if some of them had been used up, that still left an enormous number to count and gather up. He set about his task with a sigh.

Over twelve minutes later, he tapped on the door.

'Well?' snapped the teacher.

'I dunnit, sir.'

'How many?'

'Four 'undred and seventy-eight, sir.'

Soldier Stan came across to him and accepted the box. He stared into it as if conducting a count of his own then he shook his head in disagreement.

'Wrong!'

He threw the paper clips even further afield this time.

'Try again!' he ordered.

Calvin Hubberd got down on his knees once more. He realized that he would spend the whole morning picking up the paper clips. Soldier Stan would keep him at it for hours.

It was cruel and vindictive.

The Sin Bin was not what it used to be.

Chapter Three

Tariq Jahan lay on his bed with his hands behind his head and gazed upward. It was still dark enough outside to make headlights necessary and they threw strange patterns on to his ceiling as the cars turned on to the garage forecourt. He could not have slept on even if he had wanted to because the garage opened for business at six-thirty. Soon after six, therefore, Mo dragged himself out of the bed next to Tariq and stumped out of the room. Nobody had told Mo how to move silently. His lumbering gait would have woken the dead.

As it was, Tariq had stirred from his slumbers long before his brother. It was the same every morning. In the few weeks he had been there, he had not had a proper night's sleep. There was too much on his mind. Besides, every morning brought fresh hope.

Shortly after seven, he got up and tripped down the stairs. His mother was in her dressing gown, making tea in the kitchen.

'Hello.'

'Good morning, Tariq.'

'Has he been yet?'

'Who?'

'The postman.'

'Yes. The letters are on the table.'

'Anything for me?'

'Not today.'

'Are you *sure*?' he asked in hurt tones.

'See for yourself.'

'I will.'

He ran into the living room and snatched up the letters from the table. There were six of them. Four looked like bills and were addressed to his father. A long brown envelope belonged to Mo. The last letter was for Soraya. When he saw the Glasgow postmark, he felt a stab in his heart.

His mother chose the moment for a word with him.

'Tariq . . .'

'Yes?'

'You upset your father on Monday.'

'I meant what I said.'

'But you *can't* go back,' she argued. 'We need you here.'

'You could manage without me.'

'This is your family. We stay together.'

'I know that but – '

'Your father will be very angry with you.'

Tariq shrugged. It was hopeless. They all expected so much of him. He had been born into the family and had to abide by its rules. There was no point in trying to tell his mother the real reason why he was so keen to get back to Scotland. She would not understand. Nobody would.

'We love you, Tariq,' she said, giving him a kiss.

'I don't like it here.'

'Neither do we but then we did not choose this garage. They sent us here. It was nice in Glasgow but that garage was losing money. When they closed it down, they promised to find us somewhere else.' She gave him a sad smile. 'It's better than nothing. At least, we have a roof over our heads.'

'But all our relatives are in Glasgow.'

'I know.'

'And all our friends.'

'We can keep in touch with them.'

'It's not the same.'

'Tariq,' she said softly. 'It's the way it has to be.'

He nodded solemnly then moved away. Running up the stairs, he went back to his bedroom and reached under the pillow for his wallet. He took out a small photograph and stared at it for a long time. It filled him simultaneously with joy and despair.

He had written three letters to Glasgow already.

When would he get a reply?

'Best thing is English with Thin Lizzie.'

'Who's she?'

'Fattest woman on the staff,' explained Munni with a giggle. 'But she's great. You'll like her. We have some fun in her lessons.'

'What's next?'

'Maths with Wally.'

'Who?'

'Wally Walters. He's hopeless. We send him up rotten. I feel sorry for him sometimes but he asks for it.' Munni shrugged. 'Wally is a wally. That's all there is to it.'

Munni was a pretty but rather shapeless girl whose long black hair was kept in place by red slides. She loved to rattle on but Soraya did not mind that. Munni was a friend and the new pupil was grateful to her. It was wonderful to have someone who could teach you the ropes.

Soraya consulted her timetable again.

'Then we've got Mrs Lambert,' she noted.

'Watch out for old Lambo!' cautioned Munni.

'Why?'

'She's like Soldier Stan in a skirt. Dead strict. She rules the science lab with a rod of iron. Funny thing is, I like her. Lambo's always been fair with me.'

They were in the girls' cloakroom before the day's

33

lessons began. Soraya was being introduced to the members of staff she had not already met. It was strange having to get used to so many new teachers, especially in a term when she would be sitting the GCSE examination. The move from Glasgow had disrupted her education at a crucial point. But she accepted it. There was a faint air of resignation about almost anything that Soraya did.

The two girls made their way to the classroom. They had adjacent desks at the back. As they began to unload their bags, Soraya recognized two faces that came in through the door. It was Pancho Reeves and Mike O'Brien. She turned away from them.

Munni lowered her voice to a conspiratorial whisper.

'Ignore them, Soraya.'

'I'm trying to.'

'They push everyone around.'

'They're horrible.'

'Yeah,' agreed the other girl. 'Nasty pieces of work. I preferred Mark and his mates.'

'Mark?'

'Mark Stavros. He used to run 5B before them.'

'What happened to him?'

'Haven't you heard? Well, no, how could you? It was just before Christmas. The police caught them.'

'Police!'

Soraya was at once alarmed and intrigued. Munni relished her role as the class know-all. She passed on the juiciest piece of scandal with a smile playing around her lips.

'They broke into the school one night.'

'Here?' Soraya was shocked. 'What for?'

'Fun. And so that they could nick some equipment. There were four of them. Mark, Pug Anderson, Elroy

Cooper and a boy from 4C. The three from our form got youth custody. That's why they're not here now.'

'I see.'

'And that's why Pancho and Mike took over. They kept their traps shut when Mark and his mates were around. Now it's different. They're in charge. And they don't like *us*.'

'We found that out.'

Soraya sneaked a glance at the two bullies. Pancho was chewing gum as he chatted with Mike. They had a lordly manner as if the whole class owed them some kind of obeisance. Clearly, they enjoyed throwing their weight around.

A thought struck Soraya and she faced Munni again.

'The fourth boy was from 4C, did you say?'

'That's right.'

'What happened to him?'

'He got off more lightly because they said he'd been led astray by the others. Quite right, too. Anyway, he's on probation.' Munni grinned. 'Hey, your brother is in 4C, isn't he?'

'Yes.'

'Then he'll get to meet Iggy.'

'Who?'

'The boy who broke in here. Ian Higgins.'

Don Sheen never thought he would live to see the day when he was grateful to Anthea Craig. The deputy head was not one of his friends. She was unfailingly pleasant to him and always showed an interest in his work but he sensed her reservations. Mrs Craig was a traditionalist. She liked to cling to the old ways. In her opinion, some of Don's ideas were dangerously modern. It was one more reason to give her a wide berth.

35

That morning, however, it was different.

'Mr Parsons did not really think it through.'

'You surprise me,' said Don with irony.

'It's all very well appointing Mr Stanley to the Annexe but he can't just abandon his classes at the main school. He is the Head of Geography, when all is said and done.'

Mrs Craig called at the Sin Bin with glad tidings. Soldier Stan would not, after all, be there throughout each day. With exams looming at the end of term, it was essential that he kept up with his fifth and sixth year commitments. Everything else could be rejigged. What it boiled down to was that Soldier Stan would spend every morning at the Annexe and fit his other teaching into the afternoons. Having caused a complex timetabling problem, Froggy Parsons handed it over to his deputy to sort out.

The long-suffering Mrs Craig explained it all to Don.

'I hope this won't throw you out, Mr Sheen.'

'Oh, no,' he said, barely able to conceal his delight.

'Mr Stanley was so keen to come here, you see.'

'I gathered that.'

'He has very definite views about the Annexe.'

'Don't I know it!' murmured Don.

'Anyway,' resumed Mrs Craig, 'from now on, you'll get daily doses of Mr Stanley and a rota of support staff. It will mean a lot of chopping and changing but there's no help for that.'

'You mentioned support staff?'

'Yes. Three main ones.'

'Who are they?'

'Miss Finch. Mr Worthington. And Mr Riddle.'

English. French. Music. Three subject teachers were being drafted in. That was all to the good. Don had always argued for a wider spread of staff at the Sin Bin. These three had a lot in their favour. Thin Lizzie was an English

teacher with the gift of enthusiasm. Peter Worthington –
though nearing retirement – could still make the French
language sound appealing. And even Ernie Riddle, the mad
music teacher, had his good points.

All three of them were a major advance on Soldier Stan.
Mrs Craig beamed at him with her usual benevolence.

'I'll let you get on with it, then, Mr Sheen.'

'Thank you, Mrs Craig.'

'And I'll see you on Friday afternoon.'

'Friday?'

'Oh, didn't I mention it to you?'

'Mention what?'

'That was the one time-slot we couldn't cover.'

'No matter.'

'Everyone is tied up in the main school.'

'I'll hold the fort alone, Mrs Craig.'

'Oh, there's no need for that.'

'What do you mean?'

'I will be putting in a stint myself.'

'*Here*?' Don was amazed.

'Yes,' she said easily. 'We do tend to look upon the
Annexe as a colonial possession. It's high time I found out
what you actually do with the pupils we send here. Starting
this Friday, I'll be stepping into the breach.'

'Ah.'

'Unless you have any objection?' she said with a smile.

'No, no, none at all.'

But he did. Don could hear the alarm bells ringing
already. The loss of Soldier Stan in the afternoons was
good news. So was the acquisition of three committed
teachers. But Anthea Craig, the deputy head with a whiff
of the perfume counter?

She could be a decided liability.

37

Don Sheen sent up a silent prayer to his old partner.
'Come back, Bryn. All is forgiven.'

Tariq did not make it easy for him but the tubby boy was determined to be his friend. They sat next to each other in class. The flabby, freckled, dishevelled youth was one of the few who did not mock the newcomer. Indeed, he tried to fend off the teasing.

Iggy slowly broke down Tariq's resistance.

'You lives in thar garage, doan you?'

'Aye. Why?'

'Buys my sweets there sometimes.'

'Do you?'

'Yeah. On my way to school.' His eye kindled. 'Eh, can you gerrem cheap for your mates? Sweets and thar?'

'No,' said Tariq. 'I can't even do that for myself. My father always charges full price.'

'Pity!'

They were getting dressed in the changing room after a P.E. lesson. Tariq had proved himself to be a lithe gymnast while Iggy had waddled around as comically as ever.

'You don't like Woodfield, do you?' asked the fat boy.

'No.'

'Wass wrong with us, then?'

'Nothing, really.'

'Iss gor a lorra things goin' for it when you gets to know it,' argued the other. 'We did this play larst term. One of Shakespeare's. Dead good. I played the part of Bottom.' He chuckled at the reminiscence. 'Then we gorra soccer team that won the league this year. An' the best swimmin' club in the Midlands. You can play anythin' 'ere, Tariq. Soccer, rugby, 'ockey, badminton, tennis, volleyball. Even snooker and pool. You name it, we gorrit.'

'What about squash?' said the Pakistani with interest.

'Only for sixth formers.'

'Do you have any courts here?'

'No, bur they gor six in the sports complex.'

'Where?'

'Thar big place next to the swimming pool,' explained Iggy, gesturing with his hand. 'Juss the other side of the bus station, like.' He pulled on a shoe and tied the lace. 'Anyway, wor was so special about the other place?'

'Other place?'

'Your school in Glasgow.'

'Oh, aye.'

'Wass it gor that Woodfield 'assen?'

'Twelve hundred kids, for a start.'

'Blimey! Muss be bloomin' 'uge.'

'It is. They only built it six years ago.'

'Almost brand new, eh?'

'It had everything.'

'Includin' all your mates.'

Tariq nodded. His animation vanished and his face clouded over. Feeling sorry for him, Iggy put a hand on his shoulder.

'Doan worry. You'll find new mates.'

'Not like these.'

Tariq was gone. One minute, Iggy was actually getting through to him; now the shutters had been put back up. The fat boy was kept out again. Tariq had drifted off into a daydream.

About a certain person at his school in Glasgow.

Pancho Reeves liked being in the fifth form. The further up the school you moved, the more kids there were below you to bully. He and Mike were the bane of the lower school. Nobody was safe from their attentions. The Asian kids bore the brunt but the others were at risk as well. The two friends were a menace. As they walked across the playground, they deliberately bumped into smaller boys and knocked them flying.

It was four o'clock and Woodfield was letting them out at the end of another day. School was not yet over for Pancho and Mike, however. They had one last duty to perform. It took them round to a quiet spot behind the bike sheds. Pancho had evolved a plan.

'Wor do we do?' asked Mike.

'Like I told you.'

'Think it'll work?'

'My ideas always work, mate.'

'Yeah, sure.'

'We juss 'ave to be quick abourrit, thass all.'

They waited and watched pupils coming for their bicycles. Five minutes floated by. Mike O'Brien became restless. He looked at his watch then scratched his head.

'Is 'e definitely comin'?'

'Of course.'

''ow d'you know?'

''cos I sent 'im a message, didden I?'

'Did you, Panch?'

'One thar was bound to fetch 'im runnin'.'

'Wor was it?'

'I said 'is sister wanted 'im to come quick.'

Mike chortled. 'That'll bring 'im.'

'Then get ready,' urged the other. 'In thar doorway.'

'Leave it to me, Panch.'

He took up his hiding place in a nearby doorway.

They did not have much longer to wait. Two minutes later, the anxious figure of Tariq Jahan came hurrying around the angle of the bike sheds. Pancho Reeves stepped out to confront him.

'Where you goin', then?'

40

'To find Soraya.'

'We know where she is – doan we, Mike?'

'Yeah,' grunted his accomplice.

He came out of the doorway and moved up behind the Pakistani. Cold terror seized the boy as he realized what had happened.

He had walked straight into a trap.

Chapter Four

There was no means of escape. They had chosen the ideal place for an ambush. It was only twenty metres away from the bike sheds and yet it was completely out of sight. Masses of people were within earshot but Tariq could not cry out. That would be a sign of fear and he resolved to show none. Besides, he did not believe that anyone would come to his aid. The reason that bullies succeeded was that most people walked away from them and pretended that nothing was happening.

Pancho Reeves grinned broadly. His plan had worked.

'We're 'avin' a collection,' he said.

'What for?' asked Tariq warily.

'Charity. For deprived fifth formers. Mike and me.'

'So dig deep,' instructed the other boy.

'Come on,' snarled Pancho. ''ow much you gor on you?'

'Nothing.'

'He's lyin', Panch!'

'Berra nor be. I doan like bein' messed around.'

'I've got no money,' said Tariq honestly.

Pancho sized him up then came to a speedy decision.

'Less search 'im.'

'Right!'

Mike grabbed the boy from behind and held his arms. Tariq struggled but he could not shake off the bigger youth. Pancho, meanwhile, frisked him and found the wallet in his pocket. He pulled it out with a yell of triumph.

'Wor 'ave we gor 'ere, then?'

'Give it back!' insisted the owner.

'Smart wallet,' noted Pancho. 'Real leather.'

'It's mine.'

'You'll gerrit back. When we've taken wor we want.'

But Pancho was disappointed. When he opened the wallet, it was almost empty. There was no money in it at all. He pulled out various cards and pieces of paper. Then his hands closed on the photograph of a young Pakistani girl. He smirked at Tariq.

'You're a dark 'orse, mate.'

'An' a dark arse,' added Mike with a guffaw.

Pancho held up the photograph and dangled it in the air.

'See wor I found? Iss 'is bird.'

'Don't you touch that!' protested Tariq.

'Try and stop me.'

The challenge was taken up at once. Roused by the sight of his precious photograph, Tariq found extra strength to shrug off Mike O'Brien. He lunged forward to grab his wallet and his photograph then he swung a punch with all his force. It caught Pancho completely off guard and connected with his eye. He let out a cry of pain.

'You little sod!'

But Tariq was no longer there. Seeing his chance, he sprinted back to the bicycle sheds and disappeared from sight. They had no money, no victim and no pleasure.

Pancho's eye throbbed with pain. His pride had been hurt and his plan had been foiled. It would not do his image any good at all if it became known that a Pakistani fourth former had got the better of him. As the eye became puffed and discoloured, one thought dominated his mind.

Revenge.

'I'll *kill* him!'

He meant it.

* * *

Basher Bowen was stretched out on the sofa with his leg up on a stool. His plaster cast had been liberally autographed by friends and his eight year old daughter had drawn a picture of a mountain down which a matchstick man was tumbling. Basher felt that that was rubbing salt into the wound.

'Sure I'm not disturbing you, Bryn?'

'No, mun. Lovely to see you.'

'Just dropped in to see how the patient is.'

'Dying of boredom.'

Basher was delighted that Don Sheen had called in. His wife brought in some cans of beer then left them alone. They settled down with their drinks for a good natter.

'So how's it all going?' asked Don.

'No change. Leg still hurts like blazes.'

'What do you do with yourself all day?'

'Watch telly.' Basher clicked his tongue. 'Dieu! I never seen the daytime programmes before. They're murder. Especially those Australian soaps. Why import all that when we got plenty of first-class rubbish of our own?'

Don was pleased to find his colleague in such a robust mood. The Welshman's craggy face had its old colour back. He was evidently in some discomfort but his spirits were high.

'What's the latest at school?' he said.

'Don't think I dare tell you, Bryn.'

'Why?'

'Harry Stanley's taken over your duties.'

'What? Soldier Stan? He'll have the kids square-bashing in the backyard. Poor dabs.'

'Fortunately, he's not there all the time.'

He explained the situation and Basher was amused.

'Nice to know it's so difficult to replace me.'

'I miss you there, Bryn, that's for sure.'

44

'You're not the only one, Don.'

He waved a hand towards the sideboard and the mantel-piece. Both were covered with get-well cards. Another half a dozen stood on the television set and there were still more on the piano. The living room of Basher's modern semidetached house had been turned into a glorified card shop.

'Who sent them all?' wondered Don.

'Who else?'

'The kids?'

'Yes,' said Basher, with evident pride. 'Remarkable when you think about it. I mean, I'm supposed to be the Iron Man of Woodfield. Daro! They *pay* me to be unpopular. Yet as soon as I get laid up, the cards roll in like it's Christmas. Kids are funny like that.'

'They all want to know how you are.'

'Funeral's next Monday,' joked the Welshman.

'We'll be there.'

They sipped their beer and chatted about Woodfield. Given an extended holiday on medical advice, Basher could think only of getting back to his job. The Sin Bin was at the forefront of his mind. It was his way of life.

'Got many there at the moment?'

'Only the old lags,' said Don.

'Things'll soon pick up.'

'Calvin Hubberd is back.'

'*Again*? What's the little so-and-so been up to now?'

'Swilling paint across the art room floor.'

'I'd have rubbed his nose in it.'

'That's exactly what Harry did too. In a manner of speaking.'

He told Basher about the sequence with the paper clips. The Dean of Discipline shook his head in disbelief. His beetle brows were arched with concern.

'Now that is going over the top, Don.'

'I tried to tell him that.'

'Next thing you know, he'll have the kids digging holes and filling them up again. Useless, repetitive labour. What's that supposed to do for them?'

They chuntered on for a couple of hours. Basher was alternately disturbed and reassured by what he was hearing. Soldier Stan's capers were unsettling but it was good to hear that other teachers were to be given a taste of the Sin Bin as well. They would realize what a difficult job he and Don had.

'I'm just sorry I'll miss the sight of Anthea there,' said the Dean of Discipline with a chuckle. 'She'd be much better off opening a flower show than coping with our criminal fraternity.'

'Kids have got a new nickname for her.'

'What is it?'

'Sweetness and Light.'

'That just about sums her up. How's her scent these days?'

'Overpowering.'

'She ought to go in for the Eurovision Pong Contest.'

They exchanged a laugh then it was time for Don Sheen to make a move. Basher thanked him for coming and told him not to worry because the Sin Bin only had its nucleus of regulars.

'It'll soon fill up with more interesting cases.'

'I hope so.'

'Leave it to Froggy. He keeps us well supplied. Won't be long before he has some other unlucky sod on the carpet.'

His words were prophetic.

* * *

Tariq Jahan stood in front of the headmaster's desk and listened to the charge that was read out against him. Pancho Reeves was beside him, smouldering with anger and sporting a magnificent black eye. Also in the room was a stocky, middle-aged man in an overall. It was Charlie, the school caretaker. He was the star witness.

'As I came round the corner, I saw them, Mr Parsons.'

'Doing what?'

'Fighting,' explained Charlie. 'This lad here fetches that one there a punch to the eye. You can see the result.'

'It wassen a fight, sir,' denied Pancho sourly.

'You were *seen*, boy,' said the headmaster.

'I only hit him once,' added Tariq.

'Fighting is fighting,' insisted Froggy, with his first desk-thump. 'I will not tolerate it. You, Reeves, should know better.'

'Yeah, sir.'

'Just like your brother! Wilful and wayward!'

'If you say so, sir.'

'Don't be impudent, boy.'

'No, sir.'

'And wipe that sneer off your face!'

Froggy used his fist like a gavel and slammed it down on the desk again. It was time to pronounce sentence.

'Report to Mr Stanley at once.'

'Aw, sir!' whined Pancho.

'Get on with it.'

'Bur iss nor fair!'

'The Ainsley Annexe. Two weeks.'

'You carn send me there, sir.'

'Would you rather Mr Stanley came to fetch you?'

Pancho thought it over then capitulated. Soldier Stan was bad enough when he was quiescent. If he had to come looking for one of his charges, he would be in a foul mood.

Pancho was not prepared to risk that. He glared at Tariq through the eye that remained open then spun on his heel. The door slammed behind him.

Froggy Parsons addressed himself to Tariq.

'Now, Jahan. I want the truth.'

'Truth, sir?'

'*Why* did you fight Reeves?'

'I can't tell you, sir.'

'I must know, boy. Now don't prevaricate.'

'It's personal, sir.'

'Did he provoke you with racial abuse?'

Tariq was jolted. He did not want to be drawn into any explanation. If there was a punishment, he was ready to take it. He was not going to talk about the bullying or the threats or the demand for money. Still less was he ready to say anything about his beloved photograph. That was an intensely private matter. Even his family did not know the full story there.

In the face of his silence, Froggy became irritated.

'This is very foolish behaviour!' he declared.

Another two minutes passed. His anger swelled.

'I will not permit dumb insolence at this school!'

'Dumb insolence?' asked Tariq, genuinely baffled.

'Don't be smart with me, boy!'

'No, sir.'

'Be quiet!'

The headmaster jumped to his feet and did a circuit of the study with his hands behind his back. He was brooding. Charlie watched hopefully. Nothing pleased the caretaker more than to report erring pupils and to see them being punished. The problem was that he was an unreliable witness. He had not been aware of all that went on. Charlie arrived on the scene when Tariq was in the act of swinging

48

his punch. The boy was caught by this circumstantial evidence.

Froggy returned to his desk, still fuming. He gave Tariq one more chance to speak in his own defence.

'Did Reeves attack you?'

'I can't say, sir.'

'Was that other boy involved in any way?'

'Who, sir?'

'O'Brien of 5B. Did they set on you together?'

'I can't say, sir.'

'Don't be so exasperating!'

'Sorry, sir.'

Froggy breathed heavily through his nose then he clapped his hands together. He had reached a verdict.

'You leave me no alternative. The Ainsley Annexe.'

'Yes, sir.'

'Do you know where that is?'

'No, sir.'

'Do you know *what* that is?'

'No, sir.'

'You soon will.' He turned to the caretaker. 'Will you please take him across there now? To Mr Sheen.'

'Right you are,' said Charlie, glad to be instrumental in sending another miscreant to the Sin Bin. 'How long for, Mr Parsons?'

'One week.' Froggy addressed the boy again. 'I'm being lenient because you have only just come to Woodfield. But don't make the mistake of thinking I am a soft touch.'

Tariq was bewildered. When he rolled up at school that morning, he had been hauled straight off to the headmaster with Pancho Reeves and subjected to an interrogation. Now they were sending him off somewhere.

He had no notion of what might lie in store for him.

It was perhaps just as well.

* * *

49

Soraya was in a state of anxiety all through the first two lessons. Her brother had said nothing at all to her about the attack on him the previous afternoon. When he was dragged off to the headmaster's study, therefore, she was mortified. What could he possibly have done wrong? During the break, she found out.

'A fight?' she said in alarm. 'When?'

'Yesterday,' explained Munni.

'But Tariq went home with me. There was no fight.'

'According to Charlie, there was.'

'Who?'

'The caretaker. He sees everything round here.' She giggled. 'Tariq did well. He gave Pancho Reeves that lovely shiner. About time someone stood up to that bully.'

'But where's my brother now?'

'The Sin Bin.'

'*Where*?' asked Soraya.

'It's that house just down the road,' said Munni chirpily. 'It's where they send the troublemakers for treatment.'

'What kind of treatment?'

'The worst kind.'

Soraya felt faint. How had Tariq got himself into such trouble? Why had he not mentioned it to her? Who would be in charge of the treatment at the Sin Bin?

Would her brother survive?

Pancho Reeves used the long-handled broom to brush the yard. It was tedious and back-breaking work but he kept at it. Soldier Stan had him under surveillance. When the boy finished, the teacher came out to him to inspect the results. He was not impressed.

'You've missed that corner, Pancho.'

'Sorry, sir.'

'Do it again.'

'Yes, sir.'

'I want this Annexe to be as clean as a new pin.'

'Yes, sir.'

'When you've finished with the broom, you can have a crack with the scrubbing brush.'

'The *what*, sir?' wailed Pancho.

'You heard, lad,' said the teacher with a grim smile. 'I want you down on your hands and knees with the scrubbing brush until those paving slabs gleam. Is that quite clear?'

'Yes, sir.'

'Then jump to it!'

Pancho set to work with the broom once more. He had been sent to the Annexe for fighting. Soldier Stan had devised a punishment to fit the crime. He would take all the fight out of him.

Pancho Reeves was in for two weeks of hell.

Tariq Jahan had so far got off much more lightly. Don Sheen took him upstairs to the smaller classroom and set him an essay. He was one of four boys scribbling away on feint-lined paper. It was not all that different from being in the main school. But he sensed that there was worse to come.

While his class were busy writing, Don slipped out to use the telephone to contact the main school. Tariq interested him. He wanted more details from the headmaster. Everything he heard made the boy sound more intriguing. If he had really stood up to Pancho Reeves, then he deserved congratulations instead of a week in the Sin Bin. On the other hand, Don was aware of a deep hostility. The boy had a definite grudge against Woodfield. His first job would be to find out why.

Froggy's voice croaked at the end of the line.

'There is one other thing . . .'

'Yes, Mr Parsons?'

'He has a sister in 5B. Soraya.'

'That's a bit tough on her, isn't it?'

'Tough?'

'Yes,' said Don. 'Changing schools just before she does her GCSE. Couldn't they have hung on for one more term to give the kid the best possible chance?'

'Ours not to reason why, Mr Sheen. Besides . . .'

'Go on.'

'Well, girls don't rate as highly as boys in the Muslim culture. Her education may not be a prime consideration.'

'It ought to be,' insisted Don.

'How many times have I said that to Asian parents?' sighed the headmaster. 'But they have their own ways and they stick to them. Let me know how Jahan gets on, won't you?'

'Sure.'

'Goodbye.'

'Cheers.'

Don replaced the receiver and went back into the classroom. Three of the boys had used his absence to take a rest but Tariq was still writing away. The others quickly resumed. Don sat at the table and got on with some marking. He was soon interrupted.

Tariq Jahan had his hand up.

'Please, sir, may I be excused?'

'Don't be long.'

The boy got up and hurried out.

When he went across to the boys' cloakroom, he did not see the figure at the bottom of the stairs. But that person saw Tariq. It was Pancho Reeves and he could not believe his luck. An hour with the scrubbing brush had exhausted him but he felt his adrenalin flowing again now. This was his chance. Revenge was at hand. He was on his way to the cloakroom to get fresh water for his bucket. Pancho could kill two birds with one stone.

Tariq would not escape this time.

He bounded up the stairs and moved to the door. Weird noises halted him. He put his ear to the timber. Strange chanting sounds could be heard. Pancho was mystified. Twisting the handle, he opened the door and surged into the cloakroom.

What he saw stopped him in his tracks.

Tariq Jahan was kneeling on the floor and facing east. As he chanted once more, he raised his hands up then bowed forward again so that his forehead touched the carpet.

Pancho's ire returned. He got ready to strike.

But Don Sheen appeared at his elbow just in time.

'How would *you* like to have your prayers spoiled?'

The boy with the black eye seethed with disappointment. Tariq had got away again.

Chapter Five

Even during the slacker periods at the garage, there was always plenty to do. Mo Jahan tidied up the forecourt, checked the levels in all the tanks, rang the supplier to order a delivery of two-star petrol then set about restocking some of the shelves in the shop. His father had decided to widen the range of items sold. In addition to sweets, cigarettes and soft drinks, the Ace Garage now offered its customers milk, bread, rolls, biscuits and ice cream. The local evening paper was also on sale.

Mo Jahan was a carbon copy of his father except that he had a full head of hair. He had the same build, the same cast of features and the same expressions. He had also inherited his father's capacity for hard work and he kept himself busy. It was now mid-afternoon. In another hour or so, people would be driving home from work and business would be brisk.

When a battered old Vauxhall Cavalier pulled up at one of the pumps, he gave it only a cursory glance. The driver got out, unscrewed the petrol cap and helped himself to some fuel. It was the banging noise that alerted Mo. When he looked out through the window, he saw that the customer was tugging the roll of tissue paper out through the nozzle of the metal dispenser. Tearing it off in great swathes, he was making the dispenser rattle.

He used some of the paper to wipe his windscreen, another piece to clean the area around his petrol cap and a third wodge to blow his nose. He even tied some of it to his aerial so that it could act as a streamer.

54

Mo watched him carefully and feared trouble.

The customer sauntered over towards him. As soon as the young man came into the shop, Mo could smell the beer on his breath. He should not have been driving a car at all. Mo smiled politely. His father had drummed it into him that he had to be pleasant to customers even when they themselves were unpleasant.

'Good afternoon, sir.'

'You Mr Ace, then?'

'What?'

'You know,' said the customer with a grin. 'Ace Garage.'

'Oh, that's the name of the petrol, sir.'

'Thought it might be yours as well.'

'Why?'

'Well, let's face it, mate. If you was a little bit more sunburned, you'd be a kind of Ace of Spades. Gerrit!'

He laughed inanely at his own offensive joke.

'What can I do for you, sir?' asked Mo, trying to keep calm.

'Lemme see now. Four gallons of Paki petrol. Two pints of Paki oil. Oh, yeah, an' I'll take a packet of them Paki fags on the shelf there.' He threw a crumpled twenty pound note on to the counter. 'Will thar cover the damage?'

Mo controlled his anger, gave the customer his cigarettes then found him some change in the till. The young man put his face close to the window so that his nose was flattened against the glass. He gave a wild grin. With his long hair and his bandana, he looked even more like an Apache now.

'Great service round 'ere,' he said. 'Ace!'

'Thank you, sir.'

Graham Reeves let out a loud animal howl.

'Geronimo!'

He belched crudely then sauntered back out to his car.

Atlas Jahan came hurrying in from the living room to see what was going on. He watched through the window as the Cavalier started up and roared away from the forecourt. Then he turned to his elder son.

'We don't have to put up with that sort of thing.'

'I know.'

'Next time he shows up, refuse to serve him.'

The Ace Garage had its standards.

Because Woodfield Comprehensive School was also a Community College, its facilities were always in use. The children might go home at four o'clock but there was an extensive programme of evening classes on each weekday. Like many of his colleagues, Don Sheen earned some extra money by taking one of the classes. It was on psychology.

He wandered into the staff room at the main school, served himself a cup of tea and searched for a friendly face among the people already there. Thin Lizzie smiled up at him and he went over to join her. She was a big, buxom young woman in a billowing skirt and a white blouse. Her course that evening was on Drama from Ibsen to Arthur Miller. Elizabeth Finch was the livewire in the English department. Don liked her forthright manner and her unquenchable zeal for her work.

'Back to the grind,' he moaned.

'I know,' she said. 'I left my flat at eight o'clock this morning and I won't get back till after ten. Who says that teachers are featherbedded?'

'Not me, Liz.'

'It's sweated labour.'

'That's why we like it so much.'

'Anyway, enough of that,' she continued. 'How's it all going at the Sin Bin?'

'We're ticking over.'

'Can't wait for my visit there tomorrow.'

'You'll enjoy it.'

'I'll need some tips from you, Don.'

'Just play your normal game.'

'How many kids have you got?'

'Very few really,' he explained. 'A hard core of our old dependables, that's all. Then there's Calvin Hubberd. And two others who joined us today.'

'Who are they?'

He told her about Pancho Reeves and Tariq Jahan. She was sad to hear that a new pupil had got himself sent to the Annexe so soon. She had already taught Soraya and liked her immensely.

'What's the brother like?' she asked.

'I can't quite work him out, Liz. But he gave me one shock.'

'Oh?'

'I got them to write an essay on what they saw themselves doing in five years' time. Standard ploy of mine. They invariably give themselves away. The boys always want to be pop stars or disc jockeys while the girls fantasize about being models or running a boutique. None of them *ever* wants to be a teacher.'

'What about Tariq?'

'That's how I got my shock.'

'Brilliant essay?'

'Far from it. The grammar went haywire and he can't spell for toffee. But . . .'

'Well?'

'That kid certainly knows what he wants to be.'

'Prime Minister?'

'A professional squash player.'

'Is there a living in that?'

'Apparently,' he said. 'If you get to the top. And Tariq is determined to do that. He's got it all planned out in detail. Pakistan has got a tremendous record in the sport. The current World Champion is a Pakistani and their national squad has won the World Team Championships the last four times in a row. Tariq has definitely got tradition on his side.'

'But can he play, Don?'

'Oh, yes. According to his essay, he's a ranked player in Scotland. Beats kids years older than him. He looks like a beanpole but he must have talent. And he has the ambition to go with it.'

Thin Lizzie smiled her approval. It was not often that the Sin Bin threw up a potential champion.

She made a mental note to look out for Tariq.

Soraya Jahan had one major fault. She was too honest. It was almost impossible for her to keep a secret because the guilt showed in her face. Tariq hoped to conceal from his family that he was in disgrace at school and he urged her to go along with the deception. But she let herself down and the truth soon emerged.

Predictably, their father was less than pleased.

'This is very bad!' he thundered.

'Sorry,' murmured Tariq.

'It is bad that it happens and bad that you try to hide it from us. Our name is involved here, Tariq. This is bad for the whole family.'

'It was not his fault,' argued Soraya.

'We run a business here,' stressed Atlas. 'We have to be nice to people. Friendly and reliable. If you get a reputation as a wild boy, what will that do for us?'

'Explain what happened, Tariq,' urged his sister.

'What's the point?'

'They were bullying you.'

'I know it is difficult at a new school,' said Atlas. 'But you just have to make more effort. It's not much to ask.'

'Yes, it is,' whispered Tariq.

'Don't mutter behind my back!' exploded his father. 'Mo was a credit to us at school. Soraya always gets good reports. Why must *you* let us all down?'

'I've said I'm sorry.'

'You think it is all over as easy as that? You say you are sorry and we forget about it? No, Tariq! You can not shrug this off. We've been hurt. This is a stain on our family. They punish you at school and so I punish you at home.'

'Father – '

'Go to your room.'

'I just want to say that – '

'Go to your room, boy! We don't want you here.'

It was worse than the slap across the face. Tariq was being rejected. His mother and sister looked on helplessly. Their sympathies were with him but they could not intervene. The head of the family had spoken.

As Tariq got up from the table and left the room, he felt more lonely and deserted than ever. He had to get away somehow.

Pancho Reeves and Mike O'Brien shared a plastic flagon of beer. Both were smoking heavily and munching their way through packets of salt and vinegar crisps. Pancho's parents had gone out for the evening so the friends got together in front of the television. Half-watching a video of a James Bond film, they reviewed the day.

'It was deadly!'

'Sounds like it, Panch.'

'Thar Soldier Stan is a bloody sadist. I reckon 'e muss 'ave done his trainin' in one of them Jap prisoner-of-war camps. Stood over me till the sweat was comin' off in gobs.'

'Where was Jahan?'

'Upstairs with Don Sheen.'

'The soft option.'

'An' *why*, thass wor I asks?' demanded Pancho. 'I gets the black eye and 'e gets orff the best. Iss out of order, Mike.'

'Yeah. Froggy's round the twist.'

'Flamin' demented.'

Mike O'Brien took another long swig of beer.

'So wor we gonna do?'

'Gerrim!'

'When?'

'Soon!'

'Woan be easy, Panch.'

'Wor you on about?'

'The Sin Bin. They watch you every flippin' minute of the day there. You carn even turn around without 'em knowin' abourrit.'

'So?'

'There's no chance to jump 'im.'

'Who says we gorra do it at school?'

'Eh?'

'We go to 'is 'ome instead.'

'Bur we doan know where 'e lives.'

'I do, Mike. Our kid found out for me.'

'Where is it?'

'The Ace garridge on the corner of Longford Road.'

'Thar a Paki place now, is it?'

'Yeah,' said Pancho, through a mouthful of crisps. 'Our Gray dropped in there today. Lerrem know 'ow 'e felt about unwanted immigrants. 'e's good at thar.'

'Wass the next step, then?'

'Take a look for ourselves.'

'Count me in.'

'Later on, maybe.' He drained the flagon with a huge gulp. 'We'll ger some more booze on the way.'

'We'll fix thar little wog.'

'Good and proper. I owe 'im for this black eye.'

Pancho lit another cigarette and inhaled deeply. As he blew out the smoke, he allowed himself the luxury of thinking about his revenge. It would be swift and damning.

Tariq Jahan would not know what hit him.

Lunch time at the Sin Bin was a dismal affair for the inmates. They were let out into the backyard for half an hour to eat their sandwiches and mooch about. Games of any kind were forbidden. Everything was monitored by members of staff in the window above them. They were on show.

It was school with the fun taken out.

Yet it was in this unpromising arena that Tariq found another friend. As the Pakistani boy stood alone in a corner, he was joined by the gap-toothed Calvin Hubberd.

'You a mate of Iggy's, then?'

'Who?'

'Iggy 'iggins. 4C.'

'Oh, yes,' said Tariq. 'I know him.'

'Lives in my block of flats,' announced the Jamaican. 'So does Sam Jarrett. *She's* in 4C as well. An' there's a coupla others. Know wor they call our flats?'

'No. What?'

'Clearview! Iss 'cos we gorra clear view of the gasworks.'

Tariq smiled despite himself. The jaunty little character was in the main classroom at the Annexe so they did not share lessons. Calvin was no stranger to the place. He had firm opinions on how it should be run.

'Soldier Stan will ruin it,' he prophesized.

'Why?'

'Because 'e'll kill us all orff.'

'Is he that bad?'

'Gor us runnin' round like blue-arsed flies.'

'Mr Sheen doesn't hassle us at all.'

'Don is OK,' said Calvin knowledgeably, 'bur 'e will try to ger inside your 'ead. Likes psychology, see. You watch 'im if 'e arsks you in for a private chat. It'll be you, 'im an' the tape recorder. Gives me the willies, all that.'

'What about this Mr Bowen?'

'Old Basher?' The affection was unforced. 'Best of all. Knows wor kids like us need. A good kick up the arse now an' then bur a laugh or two as well. Soldier Stan duzzen know 'ow to laugh. Afraid 'is teeth'll fall out.'

They chatted away for a long time. Without noticing it, Tariq was becoming more and more relaxed. Calvin was a lively companion. He explained a lot of things about Woodfield.

The bell went to summon them back inside. The Jamaican's manner changed. He held Tariq back as the others filed out then hissed a message.

'Watch your back, Tariq.'

'Why?'

'Pancho Reeves is arfter you. Couldden say anythin' when 'e was out 'ere with us bur I can now. Pancho and Mike O'Brien 'ave gorrit in for you. They were talkin' about goin' to your garridge.'

The implications shook Tariq. He was very worried.

'Thanks, Calvin. You're a friend.'

Don Sheen was as good as his word. He honoured his promise to pass on some tips to Thin Lizzie about how to teach at the Annexe. In the event, the English teacher did not need much advice. She fashioned a lesson that worked very well. It was a version of a warm-up exercise that she used in the drama studio.

Both the groups were combined that afternoon so that Don was able to sit in as a spectator. They used the main classroom. All the desks and chairs were stacked in one corner. The dozen or so boys stood in the middle of the room, wondering what was going to happen.

Thin Lizzie soon told them. Wearing a capacious track suit and carrying a small tambourine, she took control.

'First of all, I want you all to take off your shoes.'

There was surprise and amusement at this.

'Wait,' she corrected. 'First of all, open the windows and *then* take off your shoes.' They liked that. 'Hurry up. I want you all stripped down to your socks in five seconds. Come on!'

They obeyed and put their shoes to one side. Next she got them to remove their coats. They then did a series of exercises that were designed to relax them. When she felt that the tensions had eased, Thin Lizzie made them all lie on the floor.

'OK,' she said, 'I know there's not much room so wriggle about till you're comfy. Everybody ready? Now, then – close your eyes. One eye, in your case, Pancho.'

Tariq led the laughter. He was enjoying the lesson.

'OK,' continued the teacher. 'Now I want you to think of your favourite dream. Something you'd *really* like to have come true.' Sniggers went up. 'Come on. This is serious. Think hard. Concentrate.'

Don watched with amazement. She had them in her power.

Thin Lizzie kept on talking but her voice got softer and slower and more persuasive. She was all but lulling them asleep. Some of the roughest kids in the school had become docile and malleable. It was quite an achievement.

63

'Keep thinking about those dreams,' she whispered. 'Because you're going to tell me about them. If you feel a foot touch you, start talking. When you hear the tambourine, you stop and someone else takes over. Only don't lose the thread of your dream if I halt you in the middle. I'll come back twice, three times, whatever, until each one of you has told his full story. Now float into those dreams. Don't listen to the others. Think of your own.'

She nudged the first boy with her foot.

'My dream is about goin' to America, like, an' gerrin' a job in Disney World. I'd be a sort of designer and invent new things that they'd build there. Millions of kids would come an' I'd be famous and earn lots of money and drive this great big car with my name on the numberplate. Then I'd –'

The tambourine halted him. A foot set off Calvin.

'I dream of goin' back to Jamaica as a millionaire so's I can 'ave this mansion, like, an' this fantastic yacht. I'd sail it all round the Caribbean and 'ave adventures an' thar. Yeah, an' great parties. I'd invite famous people. Startin' with –'

Simultaneously, the tambourine and toe did their job.

'Space travel,' came another voice. 'Thass wor I dream of. Iss always the same. I'm in this space rocket, like, an' I'm flyin' back to the mother ship when – BANG – it blows up. I'm the only survivor. The last 'uman bein' in space. So wor I does is this, see? I sets my course for Mars an' I –'

Tambourine. Back to Disney World for a minute.

Tambourine. On to the party on a Jamaican yacht.

Tambourine. The space traveller has another minute.

Tambourine. Pancho Reeves takes his turn.

'My dream is to rule this country as a milit'ry dictator, like. Juss me an' this 'uge Army so's everyone gorra obey me. I'd live in Buckin'am Palace an' eat orff gold dishes. The royal family would be my servants 'cos I'd be number one now. I'd parss all these laws to make Britain great again.'

Tambourine. A dream that begins on the ocean bed.

Tambourine. Another that deals with the pop world.

Tambourine. Disney World once more.

Tambourine. Pancho's fascist fantasies.

Tariq lay motionless and let his own dream fill his mind with the purity of its vision. He had dreamt it many times, awake and asleep. A nudge from a foot unlocked it.

'My dream is to escape. To run away to the Highlands of Scotland where the mountains touch the sky and the lochs are deep and wide. And when I got there, she'd be waiting for me. Wearing that same blue dress. Nobody would know where we were . . .'

Thin Lizzie brought in two new dreamers then she went back to Tariq. The tambourine did a quick round-up of all the dreams so far then collected a few new ones. Tariq had a third turn. In rapid succession, she went around the group so that all of them had launched their fantasies. By constantly moving from one to the other, she kept them all on the boil.

Don Sheen was transfixed. She had built up an amazing degree of trust and was trespassing on the innermost thoughts of some of them. Their dreams came in all shapes and sizes but each was real to the person who described it. Thin Lizzie brought them all to fruition and left Tariq until the end.

'. . . and when I won the World Championship, I'd take the cup back with me and give it to her. She'd wear the blue dress again. And we'd have this cottage in the Highlands of Scotland where the mountains touch the sky and everyone – *everyone* – would leave us alone. So we'd stay there for ever.'

The silence that followed lasted several minutes.

Chapter Six

Mo Jahan hated getting up early but he had no choice in the matter. It was his week for the morning shift. His alarm went off at six o'clock and he killed its buzz with a tired finger. Giving himself a few minutes to come fully awake, he got out of bed, clumped his way across the room and got dressed in his overalls. After going to the bathroom, he padded downstairs to the kitchen and put the kettle on for the first important cup of tea of the day. The transistor radio also came alive. Bright pop music mocked his lazy yawns.

He took the keys, went into the shop and unlocked the front door. Then he went out on to the forecourt to unlock the six petrol pumps in readiness for another day's use. It was a crisp morning with the sun fighting to shake off a blanket of white fleecy cloud. Mo filled his lungs with the fresh air and felt a lot better.

It was then that he noticed the damage. All four of the metal rubbish bins had been dented and scratched. One of the tissue paper dispensers had been wrenched from the wall. And the air hose had been tied in a series of crazy knots.

'Oh, no!' he sighed.

Petty vandalism was not a good enough excuse to rouse his father. He did what he could to rectify the damage then went back towards the shop. Another small outrage beckoned. Someone had used spray paint across one of the windows to leave a short, accusatory message.

TARIK STINKS!

They could not even spell his name properly.

Mo stood there dumbfounded for some time. Then he went through to the kitchen to get a cloth and a bottle of Windolene. It was a painstaking job but he gradually erased the words. When it was all over, he went in for a cup of tea that was now even more welcome. It tasted delicious.

Going back out to the forecourt again, he surveyed the damage. He could imagine what his father would say. His eye then travelled to the window on which the message had been left.

He decided to make no mention of it to Tariq.

His brother had enough problems as it was.

Along with his many faults, Froggy Parsons did have some virtues. Punctuality was one of them. He always arrived early at Woodfield so that he could cope with any problems that had arisen overnight, and so that he would have plenty of time to get ready for the working day. Anthea Craig usually pulled into the car park some ten minutes after him. That morning, however, she was there in advance of him. There was a lot to discuss.

They went into his study and attacked the agenda. Most of it concerned the administration of the main school but the deputy made sure that the Annexe was not ignored.

'I just wanted to raise a possibility, headmaster.'

'Raise away, Mrs Craig.'

'Well ... I hope you won't think this is disloyal of me ...'

'We have no secrets from each other,' he said, with a near-miss at a reassuring smile. 'Tell me what's on your mind.'

'It's Mr Stanley.'

'What about him?'

'I'm beginning to wonder if he really is the right man to take over at the Annexe.'

'Why do you say that, Mrs Craig?'

'I've been having a lot of feedback from there.'

'Feedback?'

'Complaints about his methods.'

'That means they must be working,' deduced Froggy. 'It's only because he's so effective that the pupils are complaining.'

'It isn't only the pupils, headmaster.'

'Oh, well, I'd hardly expect Mr Sheen to approve of him.'

'Comments have come from other quarters as well.'

'Name names.'

'Well . . .'

'Come on, Mrs Craig. If there's criticism, I want to know where it's coming from. I myself have every confidence in Harry Stanley – as I'm sure you do.'

'I certainly did, headmaster. Until yesterday.'

'What has occurred to change your mind?'

'I spoke with Miss Finch.'

'Ah!'

'And with Mr Riddle. Both were unsettled by what they found over there. Discipline is one thing but Mr Stanley has been – how can I describe it? – a trifle over-enthusiastic.'

'I regard that as a good fault.'

'So you wish him to continue his duties?'

'With my full backing.'

'Oh dear!'

'I do wish people would stop trying to undermine the fellow,' said Froggy, wagging a finger. 'He's only been there a few days. The bottom line is this : Harry Stanley accepted the assignment willingly. Would anyone else have done that?'

'Probably not.'

'Miss Finch?'

'Unlikely.'

'Mr Riddle?'

'No, headmaster.'

He peered over the top of his horn-rimmed glasses.

'Would *you* have taken it on, Mrs Craig?'

'Had it been essential – yes.'

'But would you have volunteered? As Mr Stanley did.'

'No, I wouldn't.'

'There you are, then. Case dismissed.'

He was infuriating when he was in one of those moods.

Mrs Craig backed off. Clearly she was getting nowhere and she was, in any case, relying on second-hand opinions. That same afternoon, she was timetabled to teach at the Annexe herself.

She would be able to assess the situation on the spot.

Soraya made both of them late. Because she overslept by ten minutes, she and her brother found themselves trotting along the main road towards Woodfield. It made reading her letter very difficult. The postman had once again brought something from Glasgow for her but nothing for him. Tariq was hurt.

'If you put that letter away, we can go much faster.'

'But I'm reading it,' she insisted.

'We've no got the time, Soraya.'

'It's from Zaitoon.'

'I don't care who it's from. Hurry up!'

'There's a bit in it for you.'

'We should have been there by now.' Tariq heard what she had said. 'A bit for *me*?'

'About Natasha.'

His heart missed a beat and he grabbed the letter.

'Where!'

He stopped immediately and forgot all about school. News of Natasha came before everything. He read hastily through the paragraph that concerned him and his sympathy welled up.

'Natasha has been ill.'

'That's why she hasn't written to you.'

'Glandular fever.'

'It's really knocked her about.'

'Poor girl.'

He was filled with compassion and vowed to send her a card as soon as possible. Her silence had been like a thorn in his flesh. At last there was an explanation. His spirits lifted.

They moved on down the road then split up. While Soraya ran on to the main school, Tariq crossed the road to the Ainsley Annexe. He opened the door and went in. Soldier Stan confronted him.

'You're late, boy!'

'Am I, sir?'

'Several minutes late.'

'Sorry, sir.'

'I insist on good timekeeping.'

'It won't happen again, sir.'

'I'll make sure of that. Come into my room.'

'But I'm in Mr Sheen's class.'

'Not this morning. Everyone is in with me.'

'Oh.'

Soldier Stan pointed to the open door of his classroom. Tariq felt his stomach lurch.

Munni made life at Woodfield bearable for Soraya. She helped the newcomer over the first few difficult days and was always on hand to give a word of advice. As they made their way along a corridor towards the science lab, Soraya turned to her new friend once again.

'Did you see him?' she asked.

'Who?'

'Mike O'Brien.'

'What about him?'

'He keeps looking at me in a strange way.'

'You'll have to get used to that,' warned Munni. 'He does that to all the girls.'

'This is different. Like as if he . . . knows something.'

'You mean – dark and secretive?'

'Yes. It's giving me the collywobbles.'

'Forget about Mike O'Brien.'

'I try but he won't take his eyes off me.'

'Like me to tackle him about it?' said Munni bravely.

'Oh, no. I don't want to get *you* into trouble.'

'There could be a simple answer, Soraya.'

'Could there?'

She giggled. 'Maybe he fancies you.'

'Don't say that even in fun!' gasped the other.

'I was being serious.'

'But Mike O'Brien hates Pakistanis.'

'He might make an exception for you.'

They went into the science laboratory where the experiments had already been set up. Lambo was there in her spotless white coat, giving them all a hygienic smile of welcome. Munni and Soraya went to a table halfway down the room. They were both startled when Mike O'Brien moved across to them.

He flashed Soraya a wicked grin.

'Did 'e ger the message?'

She was utterly bewildered.

* * *

71

He spent an hour or more in the corridor, picking up paper clips at the command of Soldier Stan. It was demeaning. They were often punished at his former school – even caned in rare cases – but Tariq had never been subjected to anything like this.

Two hours of classwork did not provide much relief. The teacher gave them a brief geography lesson then got them writing an essay about the country they would most like to visit. Tariq had difficulty churning out more than a few paragraphs. His mind was on Natasha. He had to send her a get-well card. The thought of her lying in bed in distress upset him deeply.

He thought about her blue dress, hanging in the wardrobe.

He remembered the school outing to the Highlands.

Soldier Stan's voice sliced through his reverie.

'What's this supposed to be?'

'My essay, sir.'

'Is that what you call it?'

'I did my best.'

'Well, it's nowhere near good enough,' said the teacher acidly. 'I've seen longer telegrams!'

'I'm a slow writer,' argued Tariq.

'Then you obviously need more time to work. See me in the main school at four o'clock. You can have an extra half hour.'

'But I can't come *then*!'

'Let's make it an hour, shall we?'

'I've got somewhere important to go, sir.'

'An hour and a half.' Soldier Stan arched an eyebrow. 'Any advance on that? Every time you argue, I'll stick half an hour on. And I don't mind if I keep you there till midnight.'

Tariq's mind was in a turmoil. The news about Natasha

had shaken him. Sending her a card that very day was a top priority but it would be impossible if he was kept in until after five-thirty. He tried to bargain with Soldier Stan.

'Let me give up my lunch break to write the essay.'

'You don't *have* a lunch break, Jahan.' The teacher held up a familiar box. 'I'd like you to count these paper clips again.'

Scotland seemed as if it were continents away.

There were some things that were beyond even Graham Reeves' skill as a mechanic. When he needed major repairs to his engine, it was time to turn to the professionals. He waited with mounting impatience while the service manager at the Vauxhall garage looked under the bonnet of the Cavalier. It took a long time to complete the estimate. Graham was sarcastic.

'Like me to come back tomorrer when you finished?'

'Almost through, sir.'

'I doan believe it!'

The service manager took out a pocket calculator and used it to add up the figures he had jotted down on his pad.

'Three hundred and ten quid!'

'*What!*'

'Engine's clapped out. Needs a lot of attention.'

'Three 'undred quid's worth?'

'Plus VAT.'

'Daylight flamin' robbery.'

'By rights, you need a new exhaust system as well.'

'That'll 'ave to wait.'

Graham studied the engine and shook his head. He had not allowed for that kind of expenditure. Yet he needed a

73

car. It had to be mended somehow. It faced an MOT test in a month.

'Well, sir?'

'Carn I knock you down by fifty quid?'

'Not if you want me to take the job on.'

'Bur I been a valued customer.'

'All our customers are valued, sir.'

'Three 'undred quid. An' 'ow long?'

'Full day's work then you'll be back on the road.'

'OK. You're on.'

'Would Monday morning suit you, sir?'

'Yeah. If you like.' He brightened. 'Juss the job, mate. Give me time to go to the bank for some cash.'

'We do take credit cards, you know.'

So did Graham. When he could get his hands on them.

Mrs Craig was quite different from any of the other teachers they had encountered at the Annexe. Peter Worthington was adequate but far from exciting. Ernie Riddle scored higher because he played music at them. Thin Lizzie was even more popular. She had really got to grips with them somehow. Soldier Stan, of course, was a walking ordeal and Don was the resident Mister Softee.

Anthea Craig was unique. After trying to asphyxiate them with her perfume, she gave them a history lesson as if she were bestowing a Christmas present upon them. Her gushing manner was remarkably effective. Most of the pupils sneered at the deputy head but she had a quality that was not shared by any of her colleagues. She was gracious.

'And now, I want you to write an essay . . .'

'Nor another one, miss!' moaned someone.

'You *are* here to work,' she reminded them. 'The title of the essay is – What Can We Learn from the Past?'

'Nothin' at all,' suggested a wag.

'Then state a case for that,' she said. 'If you believe, with Henry Ford, that history is bunk – say so. But substantiate your arguments. Start writing now.'

Amid protestations, they got on with it. Mrs Craig looked around the classroom. It contained some of the worst troublemakers in the school yet she had held their interest. That was an achievement though she was not sure that she would care to try to repeat it on a daily basis. The Sin Bin was a testing ground for educational technique. She was happy to quit while she was winning. Discipline with a human face. That was her style.

Crouched over his desk, Tariq forced his pen over the paper. He wrote in short spurts and devoted most of the time to thoughts of Natasha up in Glasgow. He missed her more than he had ever believed was possible and he hoped that she missed him. If she was ill in bed, she would need all the cheering up she could get. He elected to buy her a humorous card, something that would make her smile that special smile of hers.

It was strange. He had known her for years without paying any real attention to her. Then the school organized a coach trip to the Highlands and he went along. Natasha wore a blue dress that altered his whole view of her. She was beautiful and he had never even noticed. She was intelligent yet he had never really talked to her. Most important of all, she liked him and he had never for a moment suspected it.

One glorious summer's afternoon had transformed his life. He matured on that coach trip. He was given a focus. School then became a continuous pleasure. *She* was there and that made everything perfect. The days rolled happily by until the calamity.

Atlas Jahan had to leave his garage in Glasgow and move

to another one in the Midlands. Tariq was suicidal. How could they drag him away from Natasha? It was cruel.

'Almost four,' warned Mrs Craig. 'Finish off.'

Tariq scribbled a last sentence and sat back.

'Calvin . . .'

'Yes, miss?'

'Collect the essays in, please.'

'Now?'

'Yes.' She raised her voice over the mild hubbub. 'Make sure that your names are at the top of the papers. I don't want any anonymous essays.'

Calvin Hubberd skipped around the room and gathered up all the pieces of paper. He put them in front of her on the desk.

'Thank you, everybody,' she said. 'Goodbye.'

They did not need a second invitation. Some of them were out of the door in a flash, glad to shake the dust of the Sin Bin off their feet for a whole weekend. Pancho Reeves stayed long enough to direct a malevolent stare at Tariq then he ambled out.

There were soon only two boys left in the room.

'Tough, mate!' said Calvin.

'What do you mean?'

'I'm finished but you 'ave to start again.'

'Eh?'

'Over at the main school, Tariq. While the rest of us can gerroff 'ome, you gor another 'our an' 'alf of it.'

'Do I?'

'At least, mate. If you're nor careful, 'e'll stick on some more time as well. Watch 'im. 'e's poison.'

Tariq needed only a few seconds to reach a decision.

'I'll no go across to the main school.'

'Bur Soldier Stan's waitin' for you.'

'Let him wait!'

'Wor if 'e turns nasty, though?'

'I won't be there to see it happen.'

Tariq picked up his bag and led the way out. As they left the building, he looked across at the main school. It was not so easy to defy now that he saw it looming there. It began to exert a pull and he had to fight to resist.

Soldier Stan or Natasha? Extended misery with the teacher or the chance to send a card to his girlfriend? The choice made itself. He turned his back on the school and walked away.

Calvin's eyes burned with admiration.

He ran off to catch his new friend up.

Tariq Jahan was a hero.

Chapter Seven

Atlas Jahan was sitting behind the cash desk in the shop when he saw his daughter returning home from school. He went out on to the forecourt to greet her. His face was stern and impassive.

'Where is Tariq?' he asked.

'I'm not sure, Father.'

'He is supposed to bring you home, to look after you.'

'I can manage on my own.'

'In streets like these? You must be careful.'

'Tariq went shopping somewhere.'

'Shopping!'

'He sent his friend, Calvin, with a message. I was to come on back. Tariq won't be very long.'

'I see.'

He took his daughter by the elbow and led her across to one of the damaged bins. With a wave of his hand, he indicated the other casualties. Soraya became indignant.

'Who did it?'

'That's what I want to ask you.'

'But I have no idea, Father.'

'Don't you? I wondered if it might be someone from school.'

'School?'

'There was something sprayed on the window,' he explained. 'A message about Tariq. It was insulting. Mo cleaned it off.'

'Why should anyone want to do this to us?' she said.

'Lots of reasons.'

'It's dreadful!'

'Maybe they don't like Pakistanis.'

'We've lived in this country all our lives.'

'Makes no difference to some people.'

Soraya looked around in blank disgust. All that unnecessary damage. It was sickening. Two cars pulled up to neighbouring pumps and Atlas had to go back to his cash desk. Soraya went through to the living room where her mother gave her a kiss and a hug. Hamida was as distressed as anyone by the attack on their property.

'Who could do such things to us?'

'I wish I knew.'

It hit the girl with the force of a blow and she reeled. Something had been sprayed on the window. Her mind flashed back to the cryptic remark made by Mike O'Brien in the science lab.

'Did 'e ger the message?'

Could the boy with the broken nose be the culprit?

Her brain was racing wildly.

Pancho Reeves sat in a coffee bar in the precinct with Mike O'Brien. As they slurped their drinks, they discussed their tactics.

'I say we should have done much more.'

'Nah.'

'Take the place to pieces bit by bit.'

'Tricky. An' they'd bring the coppers in then.' Pancho spooned more sugar into his tea. 'A few little things, thass the way. Juss enough to get 'em on the raw.'

'You're the boss, Panch.'

'We wanna enjoy it, Mike. Stretch it out.'

'Yeah.'

'Next time, we'll nick some small items.'

'Like Tariq's head!'

'You said it, mate.'

The black eye was taking on a yellowish tinge now. Most of the pain had gone but the embarrassment remained. People still tended to stare at him.

'Wass it really like?' said Mike involuntarily.

'Eh?'

'The Sin Bin. With Soldier Stan.'

'Doan mention that silly sod!'

'Bad as ever?'

'I could crucify 'im!'

'Wor about the Paki?'

'Tariq?'

'Soldier Stan could eat him for breakfast.'

'Thass wor 'e did do this mornin',' recalled Pancho with a grin. 'Gave 'im the full treatment. An' iss nor over yet.'

'Issen it?'

'No. Stan's keepin' 'im in to write an essay.'

'Blimey! Could be there all bloomin' night!'

'Maybe we should 'ang around. Ger 'im on 'is own.'

They traded a sinister smile.

Harry Stanley sat in the staff room until five o'clock and did some marking. He was teaching an evening class and so he was not able to leave the premises yet. But he could do something about Tariq Jahan's failure to turn up.

He walked along to the school secretary's office, which was next door to the headmaster's study. Cleaners were just finishing off. He went into the room and opened a drawer in a desk. Extracting a large red book, he leafed through it until he found the page that he wanted. The book contained the home addresses of every Woodfield pupil.

Soldier Stan was only interested in one. Tariq Jahan. The Ace Garage.

He would find it.

* * *

80

Atlas was waiting on the forecourt when his younger son finally showed up. The father wore a look of subdued anger. Tariq was rather shamefaced. Confrontation was immediate.

'Where've you been?'

'To the shops.'

'You should have come home with Soraya.'

'I know but this is important.'

'Nothing is more important than your sister,' asserted Atlas. 'Your job is to protect her. You know what happens to girls who wander the streets on their own. Is that how you want Soraya to end up?'

'No. Of course not.'

'Then do your duty, Tariq.'

'I do, Father. Most of the time.'

'When it suits you.'

'She's my sister. I love her.'

'Show that you do.'

Under his glare, Tariq's gaze wilted.

Atlas led him across to the damaged property and his son's eyes blazed. Tariq was enraged by what he saw.

'Who was it?' asked his father.

'How would I know?'

'We think it might be someone you know. From Woodfield.'

'Why?'

'There was a message on the window. For you. I will not repeat it. Mo cleaned it off this morning.' He held the boy by the shoulders. 'Now, Tariq. Who could it be?'

'I haven't a clue.'

'Tell the truth. This is our holy day.'

'Father, I *don't* know who did all this,' promised Tariq. 'But I'll do my best to find out.'

'So will we.'

They went into the shop and through into the living room. Mo was reading the evening newspapers. Hamida was at work in the kitchen beyond. Tariq nodded a welcome and put down his bag.

'You still have not told me,' Atlas reminded him.

'Told you what, father?'

'Why you went shopping.'

'It's . . . private.'

'You are my son. There is no such thing.'

'I went to . . . buy something, that is all.'

'You have brought it home with you?'

'Uh, no. I posted it. If you must know, it was a card.'

Atlas pursed his lips and his brow furrowed.

'Who did you send this card to?' he pressed.

'A friend.'

'What was the name?'

'Does it matter?'

'What was the name!' repeated Atlas.

'Qasim.'

'Don't lie to me, boy.'

'I sent a card to Qasim in Glasgow.'

'And to nobody else?'

Once again, Tariq's gaze wilted before his father's stare. The latter's ire increased at once. He took the boy by the lapels of his jacket and shook him.

'I told you to forget her. She is not for you.'

'Father – '

'When the time comes, *we* will choose for you.'

'It does not have to be like that.'

'In our family, it does.' He released the boy and indicated Mo. 'Next year, your brother goes to Islamabad to be married. He does not complain like you. Mo respects our right of choice.'

'I trust you,' said the elder son.

'But Tariq does not.'

The boy was trapped in another blind alley. He looked around desperately for a way out but he could find none. His father wanted him to submit. Tariq himself longed to make up his own mind. Natasha was the only one for him.

Yet his family would never even consider her. There would be battles all along the way. Tariq would be outnumbered and under immense pressure to conform but he was resolved to fight for his own right to choose at whatever the cost.

He would have to hurt the people he loved most. But he was ready to pay that price

Graham Reeves collected up the last of the empty glasses and put them into the machine to be washed. After wiping the tables and the bar counter, he put everything away and took his leave. It was just after midnight.

Les and Badger were waiting for him in the car park, hunched against one of the concrete pillars. Like him, they were muscular characters in their late teens. Les had a livid scar over one eye and Badger wore a full beard.

They saw their mate strolling towards them.

'Wor kept you?' asked Les.

'Sorry.'

'We 'ad to pass up a great chance.'

'Yeah,' added Badger. 'We needed our frightener.'

'I'm 'ere now.'

'Same system?' said Les.

'Stick to a winnin' formula,' urged Graham.

'Less split up, then,' decided Badger. 'Remember that *I'm* the one who grabs the wallet. You two ger anythin' else thass goin'. OK, mates?'

They spread out and vanished into the shadows.

83

It was the largest car park in the city and it was on the fringe of the precinct. Dozens of vehicles were still waiting to be collected and the area was also used by pedestrians as a short-cut to the ringway.

If they waited long enough, something would turn up. It usually did. The secret was to know when to strike. Three youths went singing raucously across the car park. They were not fair game. Another small gang came and went without realizing that the three friends were all ready.

Their patience was eventually rewarded. A middle-aged Pakistani in a smart brown suit and flashy tie headed towards a Rover on the far side of the car park. The man was all alone and, judging by his shambling gait, he had been drinking.

Three to one. It was like taking candy from a baby.

Graham Reeves had come to make another withdrawal at his bank. He led the move as they converged on their victim.

A week was a long time in the life of Woodfield. On Monday morning, Tariq had found the place totally hostile to him. By Saturday, however, he was strolling towards the sports complex with two new friends, Iggy and Calvin Hubberd. They were going to play squash.

As they reached the main entrance, two girls came out with wet hair and shining faces. Samantha Jarrett and Melanie Judd had been swimming together. Bright-eyed and full of zest, they hailed their fellow fourth-formers and had a brief giggle. Tariq was introduced to them and liked them straight away. He now had four friends at Woodfield. Things were improving.

The boys went in, paid their money and climbed the steps to the changing rooms. Iggy looked patently absurd in squash kit but he did not mind the teasing. Calvin wore white football shorts and an ordinary white shirt so he did not look the part either.

But Tariq did. Tall, thin and sinewy, he gave off a glow of fitness. His kit was freshly-laundered and his racquet was of a much higher quality than the cheap wooden ones brought by the others. Calvin and Iggy, however, were not deterred. They followed the Pakistani down to the number one court.

Iggy claimed to have played only once or twice before but Calvin had been there quite often in the winter months. Tariq therefore challenged him first. Iggy was to take over when Calvin was exhausted then vice-versa.

'Suppose *you* ger exhausted first, Tariq?' asked Iggy.

'I don't think that will happen, somehow.'

'Fancies 'isself, doan 'e?' said Calvin.

'We'll teach 'im, Cal,' promised Iggy.

'Between the two us, we'll murder 'im.'

As soon as he got on court with Tariq, Calvin realized what an idle boast it was. He was completely out of his depth. Tariq was fitter, faster and vastly more talented. He won three games without conceding a single point.

'My turn now!' said Iggy with unabated enthusiasm.

'Good luck!' gasped Calvin, bent double to regain his breath. 'I tired 'im out for you, Ig. All yours now.'

But Tariq was still as fresh as a daisy. Iggy provided no opposition at all and the Pakistani coasted along. Once again, he won three games without dropping a point. His two friends were now near collapse and he had not yet broken sweat.

While they recovered, Tariq went through a punishing solo routine which kept him sprinting from one corner of the court to another as he retrieved his own previous shot.

Other marvels followed at will. Iggy and Calvin watched with popping eyes.

'Fantastic!'

'Boy's a genius!'

'Next world champion.'

'Wish *I* could play like thar.'

Tariq was oblivious to their presence and their comments now. He was caught up in the sport that he loved, dedicating himself to its mysteries and its challenges. Only when he was dripping with sweat and panting for breath did he give up. His performance had been quite mesmeric.

'Where d'you learn to play like thar?' said Iggy.

'On a squash court.'

''ow old were you when you started?'

'Eight.'

Calvin chuckled. 'When I was eight, I thought thar squash was a nice cool drink.'

They traded a laugh then moved back to the changing rooms. Tariq was delighted to have been back on a squash court again. It made him revalue the city to which he had come yet again. Maybe it was not such a terrible place, after all.

But his heart remained in Glasgow. Nothing would ever alter that fact.

On a busy day like Saturday, everyone in the family had to take a turn at the cash desk. Atlas, Mo, Hamida and Soraya all did their share at the Ace Garage. When Tariq got home from the sports complex, he relieved his sister and went on duty. Cars rolled in at regular intervals. He was at full stretch.

At last there was a lull in the traffic. Tariq was able to take a breather and grab a snack. He even had time to dip into a squash magazine that he had bought himself. An article about Pakistan's contribution to the game caught his attention and he was soon totally absorbed in it.

He did not see the Ford Escort roll up at one of the pumps. Nor did he notice the tall, erect, distinguished-looking man who got out to help himself to twenty-five litres of four-star petrol. The customer marched across to the shop and went on in, putting some cash down on the counter. Tariq glanced up, saw the amount of petrol that had been used and rung up the appropriate amount on the cash register.

Quite absent-mindedly, he handed over the change.

'Thank you, Jahan.'

The voice sparked off his worst nightmares.

'I was hoping to bump into you here.'

It was Soldier Stan in a natty herringbone suit.

'Hello, sir.'

'What happened yesterday?'

'Yesterday?'

'You had a detention at the main school.'

'Oh, yes, sir.'

'And you failed to turn up.'

'Sorry, sir.'

'Why?'

Tariq did not dare to tell him the real reason but no convenient lie came from his lips. He shrugged helplessly.

'*Why?*' repeated the teacher with emphasis.

'It was a mistake, sir.'

'Oh, it was certainly that!'

'I sort of got lost.'

'No, you didn't!' snapped the teacher. 'You defied me. You deliberately ignored an order from a member of staff.'

'Yes, sir,' conceded Tariq.

'It's appalling!'

'Yes, sir.'

'Did you expect to get away with it?'

'Well, no . . .'

'Actions have consequences,' boomed the other. 'You simply have to appreciate that. If you behave badly, you must be punished. If you refuse to face your punishment, then its severity must be increased. Is that reasonable?'

'I suppose so, sir.'

'Good. Let me speak to your father.'

'My father?' Tariq's trepidation swelled.

'I think he should know what sort of a son he has got. Fetch him at once, please.'

'Yes, sir.'

Tariq slipped into the living room where his father was watching some racing from a northern racecourse. There was no way that the boy could get out of it now. He had been run to ground by Soldier Stan.

'Someone to see you, Father,' he explained.

'Me?'

'From my school.'

'Who is it?'

'Mr Stanley.'

'But what does he want here?'

'To speak with you.'

'Why?' His eyes narrowed. 'Are you in trouble again?'

'I might be.'

'You'd better show him in.'

Atlas switched off the television and tidied the room very quickly. Seconds later, there was a tap on the door and Harry Stanley sailed in.

Tariq remained at the cash desk. There was no point in his being present at what was a form of trial. He could not affect the verdict either way.

The wait was agonizing. When Soldier Stan emerged, he

88

had a glint of steely satisfaction in his eyes. Atlas Jahan, by contrast, looked thoroughly cast down. He waved the teacher off then he swung around on his son.

'What's all this I hear?'

'I don't know.'

'Bad behaviour, being late, being cheeky.' A shudder passed through him. 'And now I learn that you missed an appointment with Mr Stanley as well.'

'Not on purpose.'

'I'm shocked, Tariq.'

'Something else came up.'

'You *must* do as the teachers tell you. Mr Stanley is very angry with you. He is going to see Mr Parsons first thing on Monday morning.' Atlas was shaking gently. 'How *could* you?'

'I don't know.'

'Get out of there!'

'What?'

'GET OUT!' yelled his father, quivering with rage.

Tariq obeyed at once. As he did so, the squash magazine in his hand was snatched away from him.

'And that's the end of *this* for a while,' continued Atlas, tossing the magazine into the wastepaper basket. 'No squash.'

'You can't stop me playing.'

'I can and I will. Now go to your room.'

'Father – '

'Do as I say before I lose my temper.'

Tariq gave in. With his tail between his legs, he went upstairs and shut himself in his bedroom. It had been a very gruesome experience so far.

When he got to school on Monday, it might be worse.

Chapter Eight

'They'll expel 'im.'

'Norra chance.'

'Tariq'll ger orff scot free. Gerrit? *Scot* free.'

'Big joke!'

'Fancy standin' up to Soldier Stan like thar!'

'Yeah. Missin' 'is detention.'

'Dead cool.'

Speculation was rife among the pupils of 4C. It was odd. Tariq had only been in the form for a short while yet he was claimed as a regular member. Notoriety had got him accepted.

'Stan wanted to 'ave 'im 'anged, drawn and quartered.'

'Froggy calls the shots.'

'Well, 'e's *bound* to do summit stupid.'

'I think Tariq'll ger the cane.'

'Six strokes on each 'and.'

'An' six on the bum.'

'They doan 'ave a cane 'ere any more.'

'Basher does. An' 'e uses it.'

'I reckon 'e deserves a medal.'

'Basher?'

'Tariq. Less face it. Gives Pancho Reeves thar black eye and now 'e takes on Soldier Stan.'

The boys had not liked Tariq when he joined the class. All that had changed. The Pakistani had been promoted. He was a hero.

'Bravest kid in the whole class.'

'Whole school.'

'We oughta try to 'elp 'im.'

'Wor can we do?'

'Organize a demonstration, like.'

'Sign a petition.'

'Go on strike!'

The suggestion produced a roar of laughter. It was an attractive idea though not practicable. But they were keen to help Tariq in some way. They had given him a rough ride when he first arrived at Woodfield. It was time to make amends.

'We gorra lerrim know we're behind 'im.'

'Keep Soldier Stan orff his back.'

'Send 'im food parcels.'

'Smuggle 'im out.'

'Burn down the Sin Bin.'

A huge cheer of approval went up. It was fun to make plans and talk big. And it was good to have a classmate who could unite the kids against the staff. A fifteen-year old Pakistani had really set the place buzzing.

Basher Bowen took an interest in the case as well. When Don Sheen called to see him on Monday evening, he wanted to know what had happened. There was no love lost between him and Soldier Stan. They were rival disciplinarians, never happier than when the other's methods were called into question.

'You can push some kids too far,' decreed Basher.

'That's what Harry did,' said Don.

'Tariq just couldn't take any more.'

'So he waltzes off as cool as a cucumber.'

'What was finally agreed?'

'Have a guess.'

'Twenty years in Alcatraz?'

'Worse.'

'Six weeks in the Sin Bin?'

'And the rest.'

'The whole *term*?'

'Exactly.'

'Dieu! That's bloody vicious.'

'No, it's Froggy Parsons.'

'One consolation. The kid'll have you on his side.'

'Only in the afternoons, Bryn.'

'What?'

'That was one of Harry Stanley's stipulations,' explained Don. 'Tariq was to be in all his classes so that he could give the boy "personal supervision". He'll have him in chains.'

'Haven't we got some lousy colleagues, Don?'

'They're not all against the lad. Anthea Craig spoke in his favour. So did Thin Lizzie. Tariq has fans.'

'He'll need them.'

Basher reached for his walking stick and helped himself up. He hobbled across to the table. Don was mildy alarmed.

'Are you supposed to be doing that?'

'No, mun. But I can't stay on that sofa all day.' He poured two glasses of beer out. 'Here we are.' He handed one of them to Don. 'What shall we drink to?'

'Another cock-up at Woodfield!'

They supped their beer and found it refreshing.

Don became reflective. There was another aspect to the whole affair and it needed to be taken into account.

'Tariq Jahan is a Pakistani.'

'I didn't think he was Welsh!'

'You know what those Pathan families are like, Bryn. Totally committed. They expect their kids to pull out all the stops at school. It's a matter of pride.'

'So?'

'Tariq has let the side down.'

'Life at home can't be a bowl of cherries, then.'

'I think the kid's going through agonies.'

'Is he likely to make it?'

Don Sheen considered the question for a long time.

'Not if Harry Stanley keeps riding him.'

After another night behind the bar, Graham Reeves drove home to his house and let himself in. Mike O'Brien was in the living room with Pancho. They looked pleased with themselves.

'What you two been up to, then?' asked Graham.

'Doin' our bit for international understandin',' said Mike.

'Yeah,' agreed Pancho. 'We been down the Ace Garage again.'

'Get any souvenirs?'

'One or two, Gray,' said his brother.

'We 'ad a good night,' confirmed Mike. 'Talkin' of good nights, I see you gorrin the paper.'

'Oh, thar Paki we bashed. Yeah.'

'Struck gold there,' noted Pancho. 'Wor was 'e carryin'?'

'About five hundred quid in notes. An' all this jewellery, like.' He gave a harsh laugh. 'Some people haven't got the brains they were born with. I mean, who'd walk round with *thar* much?'

'You'd be surprised,' said Mike.

'You would indeed!' added Graham. 'We rolled this bloke once, 'e 'ad the best part of a grand on 'im.'

Pancho got up and went to examine his eye in the mirror. Its early blackness was gone now and yellow was the dominant hue. The swelling had subsided so that he could now see properly.

'You oughta wear one of them pirate eye-patches,' said Mike.

'Thass it,' urged Graham. 'Arrrgh, Jim, lad!'

'Stick a parrot on your shoulder while you're at it.'

'No thanks,' said Pancho. 'Think of all them droppin's.' He looked at Mike and winked. 'Hey, shall we show 'im wor we gor tonight?'

'If you like.'

'Close your eyes, Gray.'

'OK. Gerra move on.'

Pancho raced upstairs to his bedroom and brought something back down. Graham could hear it banging on the wall.

'Ready, steady – open your eyes.'

Graham did and they widened in astonishment.

Pancho and Mike had excelled themselves.

Tiny acts of vandalism seemed to take place each night now. It was almost as if someone had launched a vendetta against the Ace Garage. It affected Atlas's sleep. He found that he got up at the same time as Mo now. They opened up together.

Coming out on to the forecourt, they looked around cautiously. What was the damage this time? A watering can had been perforated and a fire extinguisher had been stolen.

'Who keeps *doing* it?' demanded Atlas.

'We'll catch him one day.'

'It can't go on like this, Mo.'

'Look on the bright side,' advised his son. 'At least, they haven't taken anything really vital.'

Even as he spoke the words, they died in his throat.

He looked upwards and got a shock. At the top of a

long steel pole, a swinging metal sign usually advertised the name of the petrol. The sign had disappeared.

It was positively the last straw for Atlas.

'This is it, Mo. From now on we have all-night vigils!'

'That should work.'

It had to. They could not go on as they were.

Tariq Jahan entered a new and more punitive phase of his career at Woodfield. Required by Soldier Stan to report early at the Ainsley Annexe, he was forced to perform all kinds of routine tasks over and over again. The teacher was out to break his spirit and Tariq, by the same token, was determined to survive. Throughout this period, Calvin Hubberd was a lifeline.

'Anythin' you need, Tariq,' he offered, 'juss lemme know.'

'How about sudden death for Soldier Stan?'

'I'm workin' on thar.'

'Apart from that, I love it here.'

'Doan we all? The Sin Bin is the in-place to be.'

'Trouble is – we're locked in!'

'There is that,' admitted the Jamaican.

Calvin's own invincibility helped Tariq to pull through. No matter how repressive Soldier Stan's methods, Calvin always came up smiling. He was an example to them all.

In the afternoons, there was always Don Sheen to help.

'How are you coping, Tariq?'

'I get through.'

'And your family?'

'They're fine.'

'Are they still mad at you?'

'Sometimes.'

'Does it get to you?'

A short pause. 'Yes.'

'How much of Asian culture do you reject?'

'That's the trouble. I don't know,'

'Still want to go to Glasgow?'

'Yes.'

'What's stopping you?'

'The family. They need me here.'

'So you'll be in the Midlands indefinitely?'

'Wouldn't say that.'

Don probed as much as he could but there was only so much that Tariq would give away. There were still large, unknown areas of his past and experience that Don knew nothing about.

'Squash.'

'I can't play any more.'

'You can't strangle a natural talent like that.'

'I will play again one day.'

'Soon?'

'I hope so.'

'Any other sporting ambitions?'

'Who knows?'

It was all very bland and noncommittal. Don tried hard but there were closed-off areas in the boy's mind, places that the teacher was just not permitted to go yet.

It would take time.

Tariq's bad behaviour at school still weighed heavily on his father. He felt responsible for it. Unable to prevent it in the first place, he now sought to confine and subdue it as much as possible.

The boy was kept largely under covers. He no longer served in the shop and he spent most of his time confined to his room. There he was expected to continue his studies, to see the error of his ways and to pray regularly.

Atlas set the tone for all this. Hamida and Soraya were

forced to go along with it but they did not really share his strict view. His sister had some insight into his real problem.

There was a tap on his door one night.

'Tariq . . .'

'Yes?'

'Can I come in?' she whispered.

He opened the door for her and swept her in, knowing that their father would disapprove. The excitement of doing something forbidden showed in her cheeks.

'Are you all right?'

'I'm fine, Soraya.'

'I worry about you.'

'It will all work out for the best.'

'Father is not being fair to you.'

'I'm glad somebody else thinks so.' He kissed her gently on the forehead. 'Why did you come?'

'To see how you were. And . . .'

'And?'

'To show you this.'

Soraya reached up her sleeve and pulled out a letter. It was written on pink paper with a slight aroma. He was puzzled.

'Another letter from Zaitoon,' she explained.

'When did it come?'

'Second post. While we were at school. I only had a chance to open it this evening.' She cleared her throat. 'There's something in it that will interest you.'

'Why?'

'It's about Natasha again. I wrote and asked her to find out what happened to those letters you sent. To ask why Natasha didn't reply to them.'

'We know that now. She was ill.'

'It's not what Zaitoon says.'

97

'What?'

'Read it for yourself.'

Tariq unfolded the pink paper and skimmed through it until he found the relevant passage. He blinked in dismay.

'Natasha never got my letters.'

'Her parents stopped them reaching her.'

'That was cruel.'

'Perhaps they thought it was necessary.'

'Necessary?'

'You have to see it from their point of view.'

'What about *my* point of view?' he demanded. 'And Natasha's?'

'You're both still so young.'

'We're fifteen, Soraya. When our parents got married, our mother was only thirteen.'

'That was another story.'

'In what way?'

'Tariq . . .' She was nervous and tentative.

'Go on,' he encouraged.

'No. You will only hate me for it.'

'Never. Say what you were going to.'

'I'm only trying to save you further heartache.'

'So?'

'This . . . friendship between you and Natasha . . .'

'Yes?'

'It can never come to anything.'

'Soraya!'

'It can't, Tariq. Oh, I wish it could but it's impossible. The two families are against it. There's no way that it will ever grow into a marriage.'

'It already has – in our hearts.'

She took him in her arms and held him, shedding tears of compassion for him. Tariq was overtaken by a feeling of hopelessness. Even his sister was against them. They were on their own.

'Try to put her out of your mind, Tariq.'

'How can you say that?'

'It's the only way. Be brave about it.'

'I could never betray Natasha.'

'She is not for you.'

His dark eyes stared soulfully up at her. The conversation was over. They would never agree. It was fruitless to go on. She opened the door a fraction to make sure that nobody was on the landing, then she let herself out. Tariq flung himself down on the bed but he found no rest. What she had said returned to torment him time and again.

He put out the light but the darkness was no solution. It was full of phantoms that came to mock and tease him. He was there and Natasha was in Glasgow. Everybody was working to keep the two of them apart. It was disheartening.

Mo joined him not long before midnight. His brother got into the other bed and it creaked with each movement he made.

'You still awake, Tariq?'

'Yes.'

'Father will keep the vigil tonight.'

'What?'

'The forecourt. I will do it tomorrow night.'

'Oh, yes.'

'Get some sleep. Goodnight.'

'Goodnight.'

Mo soon drifted off. His breathing thickened and he rolled over to face the wall. Tariq envied his ability to drop straight off like that without hours of agonizing. Natasha popped back into his mind again. In her blue dress.

Everything was fine. He luxuriated once more in memories of the outing.

A faint scraping sound then disturbed him. It came from outside and made him sit up. Edging the curtain back, he peered out through the window. His ears had not deceived him. Down below on the forecourt, a shadowy figure was trying to drag away one of the metal bins that was fixed inside a concrete post.

Tariq got up out of bed. His father was supposed to be keeping watch but he had been up since six that morning. Fatigue had probably sent him to sleep. The boy took the responsibility upon himself. Pulling on shirt and trousers over his pyjamas, he stepped into his shoes then left the room. When he got to the bottom of the stairs, he collected the keys.

The shop was in darkness but the lamppost on the corner shed an orange light all across the forecourt. Through the window, he could make out the figure pulling away his trophy. Tariq slipped the key in the lock and turned. Utilizing the element of surprise, he then flung open the door and raced out.

Hearing the noise, the thief abandoned his bin and darted off into the shadows. Tariq went after him but he did not get very far. An accomplice was lurking behind the petrol pumps. As the boy charged past, he leapt out and hurled a metal bucket at him. Had it made direct contact, it would have knocked Tariq unconscious. As it was, it caused him only a glancing blow. It slowed him enough to let the two men get away but he was not hurt.

Footsteps pummelled the pavements. They were making a run for it. Having no chance of catching them, Tariq instead put the bucket back where it had come from and dragged the bin to its accustomed position. Satisfied that the thieves would not return, he went into the shop and locked the door.

His father was waiting for him. Grim, dishevelled, torn from his slumbers, he had watched it all from his bedroom window.

'Well done!' he grunted. 'You've done something right.'

He swung round and went back off upstairs.

Tariq had no chance to tell him that he thought he had recognized both of the figures outside.

Chapter Nine

Thin Lizzie strolled along the pavement with the sun on her back. She was wearing blue today and carrying a heavy shoulder bag that contained two sets of exercise books. Various pupils walked near or past her and she acknowledged them with a smile. A motorbike then slowed down beside her and its owner lifted his visor.

'Morning, Liz!'

'Don!'

'Quicker on two wheels.'

'Not far to walk now.'

'Let me have your bag at least.'

'That's an offer I can't refuse.'

She handed over the bag and he slipped it over his own shoulder. Then he chugged along at low speed so that they could chat as they went along.

'Had any further thoughts?' he asked.

'What about?'

'That dream session you did at the Sin Bin.'

'Only that I enjoyed it more than usual.'

'So did they.'

'Any comments?'

'Masses. Please, sir, can we 'ave more of them and less of you?' He grinned. 'Seriously, though, they loved it.'

'That's the important thing.'

'And they got something out of it. They keep asking me if dreams really tell us anything.'

'What's the answer, Don?'

'Yes and no.'

102

'That gives you two choices, anyway!'

'Some dreams do, some don't.'

'What about our batch last Thursday?'

'Wonderful. They told us an enormous amount.'

'Not always very appetizing, though,' she noted. 'Pancho Reeves as a latter-day Adolf Hitler is not *my* idea of a sweet dream.'

'What is?'

'Unlimited school holidays.'

'How did you rate Tariq?'

'Fascinating.'

'Got something special, hasn't he?'

'A stillness. An ability to concentrate.'

'I was amazed at the way he opened up. Especially with a dream sequence that was so fully realized. That girl, that place, that blue dress. They all exist.'

'No wonder he's so unhappy down here.'

'Symptoms of deprivation.'

'Yeah.'

'That was on Thursday, mark you.'

'What do you mean?'

'By Friday, he'd blown it. Tariq had the gloves on with Harry Stanley and that's never a wise thing to do. When he cut Harry's detention, the fur and hair really flew.'

'I can imagine.'

'Still, thanks for what you did.'

'Pleasure.'

'What's lined up for *this* Thursday?'

'Wait and see.'

'The kids are looking forward to it, I know that.'

'So am I.'

It would be one of the highlights of her week.

* * *

Soraya was starting to wonder if she had done the right thing. She had acted from the best of intentions but that meant nothing. The simple fact was that she had made her younger brother very unhappy by the advice she had given him. He hardly talked to her on the way to school that morning. She decided to confide in Munni during the break.

The other girl listened with great interest.

'I've heard it so often before, Soraya.'

'What?'

'That situation. Loving someone you can't have.'

'Tariq thinks he *can* have her.'

'Not an earthly.'

'That's what I told him.'

'Maybe you should have let him find it out for himself,' suggested Munni. 'Either way, he'll get hurt.'

'I tried to let him down more gently.'

'He won't thank you for that.'

'I know. Tariq's made me feel so guilty about it.'

'What's she like?'

'Who?'

'This girl from Glasgow. Natasha.'

'Very lovely. From a good family.'

'Do they have plans for her?' asked Munni.

'Oh, yes. But Tariq won't accept that.'

'He must, Soraya.'

'Never.'

'They are Pathans?'

'From Peshawar, like us.'

'He is fighting thousands of years of tradition.'

'That won't stop him,' said Soraya.

Munni grinned. 'Your brother has a will of iron.'

'He likes his own way.'

'We all do.'

'Tariq never gives up.'

'That is the kind of man *I* would like to have for my husband,' said the other dramatically.

'Is it?'

Munni thought it over and realism quickly intruded. She shook her head and giggled aloud.

'Maybe it isn't. *I'd* want to win all the arguments.'

'Then you want a weak man you can push around.'

'No!' she retorted with withering disgust. 'I'd never settle for a weak anything, Soraya. What I need is a strong, sexy man I can talk round whenever I want to. Someone who worships the ground I walk on and showers me with presents.' She giggled afresh. 'Then, of course, I'd have a husband as well!'

Soraya joined in but her laughter was edged with sadness. She was the only member of her family who understood the depth of her brother's commitment. Tariq had built everything on Natasha.

'What about you?' wondered Munni.

'Me?'

'What sort of man would you like?'

'A kind one.'

'Is that all?'

'I'll just see what comes along,' she said quietly.

Munni was touched by her serene quality and felt an upsurge of affection for her new friend. She leaned forward to kiss Soraya on the cheek and squeezed both her hands.

'Whoever he is, he'll be a lucky man.'

Harry Stanley had boasted that he would empty the Annexe in a fortnight but it did not quite work out like that. In his second week there, the numbers actually went up. Two girls were also drafted in, surly creatures from 4B who were always a handful. Soldier Stan did not amend his approach. He simply intensified it. Pupils in his classroom were subjected to even harsher methods.

Don Sheen could contain himself no longer.

'You can't run this place on fear, Harry.'

'It has to have a major part.'

'This is not a Victorian workhouse, you know.'

'More's the pity,' argued the older man. 'The Victorians had the right idea. They made those places so unpleasant that nobody wanted to go there. Workhouses had a stigma and that was a good thing as well. Shame is a powerful weapon.'

'You were born in the wrong century.'

They were sitting in the window of the upstairs room during the lunch time break. Soldier Stan was reclining in Basher's armchair as if it were his own. He was still convinced that he had been a success at the Annexe. There was the same unassailable buoyancy in his manner.

'I soon knocked this outfit into shape.'

'Oh, is that what you've done?' said Don with irony.

'I've taught them to respect their elders and betters.'

'By counting paper clips?'

'It has its place,' argued the other. 'And it's every bit as effective as your wishy-washy liberalism.'

'I dispute that.'

'Calvin Hubberd got the paper clip treatment and it brought him to heel at once.'

'What about Tariq Jahan?' countered Don. 'He went through it as well and finished up by cutting your detention.'

'He's lived to regret that!'

'But it proves that bullying them just doesn't work.'

'Jahan has been brought under control now, Don. We won't get another peep out of him. I'd bet on it.'

'Would you? What d'you say to a fiver?'

The offer made Soldier Stan's jaw drop.

Graham Reeves resented paying so much money to have his engine repaired but they had done a fine job. The Cavalier sounded much quieter and ran much more smoothly. He sped along the road, flicked on his indicator, then swung on to the forecourt of the Ace Garage before stopping with a squeal of brakes. When he saw Mo at the cash desk, he gave a derisive laugh.

Hopping out of the car, he unscrewed the petrol cap.

'Excuse me, sir!' called Mo, coming out to him.

'Wassa marra?'

'You can't have any petrol, I'm afraid.'

'Run out?'

'For you – yes, sir.'

Graham bridled. 'Wor is this! You carn refuse me petrol, you daft Paki, I knows my rights.'

'We have rights as well,' affirmed Mo. 'We don't have to serve anybody who is abusive to us.'

'I'll be real bloody abusive if you're not careful.'

Atlas Jahan came out through the shop door.

'Would you like us to call the police, sir?'

'Shove orff!'

'Goodbye, sir.'

Graham jumped into his car and started the ignition. He revved the engine then raised two fingers at Mo before driving off in a blazing temper.

Mo chuckled to himself then turned to his father.

'Know something? I enjoyed that.'

Tariq Jahan shuffled into the classroom on his own and went over to his desk. He was about to lift the lid when a voice bellowed.

'And what do you think *you're* doing?'

It was Soldier Stan, filling the doorway with his presence.

'I was just getting my book, sir.'

'Has the bell gone yet?'

'No, sir.'

'Then you've no right to be here, have you?'

'It's nearly one-thirty.'

'I asked you a question,' said the teacher. 'You should not be in here until the bell goes. Should you?'

'I'm doing no harm.'

'Don't argue, boy.'

'I need my book to take up to Mr Sheen's class.'

'That's beside the point. Rules are rules.'

'But I've no done anything wrong, sir.'

'Show me something you've done *right*, Jahan!' exploded the other. 'Heavens above, you've only been in the school five minutes and look at your track record. Fighting, disobedience, lateness, cutting a detention, lying, arguing back . . . You're a disaster!'

'That's no fair, sir,' replied the boy, stung to the quick.

'I don't have time to discuss the matter with you now. See me in the main school at four.'

'But I can't, sir!'

'And don't start all that again,' warned Soldier Stan through gritted teeth. 'Report to me in the entrance hall as soon as school finishes. And make sure you be there, Jahan. If you don't, I'll come looking for you.'

The teacher marched out but his threat hung in the air.

Tariq felt his anger begin to surge.

Froggy Parsons looked around the display of cards with surprise. Almost every available surface in Basher's living room was covered and a large scroll dangled from the mirror over the mantelpiece. The headmaster was impressed and not a little envious. When he had been away from school with flu the previous term, not a single card had come from a pupil.

'Half of Woodfield must have written,' he noted.

'Only half of 'em *can* write.'

'They all want you back obviously.'

'Don't you believe it, mun,' said Basher with a chuckle. 'They're not all get-well cards. A few of them are stay-ill or get-worse cards. There's even a drop dead, sir from one joker. My favourite is that scroll on the mirror.'

Froggy took a closer look at it. The scroll bore a cartoon of a climber at the top of Mount Everest. One of his legs was encased in plaster and he was in the act of planting the Welsh flag on the summit. The message was in bold lettering – GET WELL THEN GO TO HELL!

The headmaster was outraged. He pointed a trembling finger.

'This is on school art paper!'

'You can't expect the kid to buy his own.'

'It's theft! As for the insult to a member of my staff, it's intolerable.' He stamped his foot on the carpet. 'Don't worry, Mr Bowen. I will track this boy down and punish him. This kind of ridicule must not be permitted at Woodfield.'

'It's only meant in fun,' said Basher easily.

'Fun! It's shameful!'

'I think it's great, mun. You've got to admit it's a terrific likeness of me. I love those eyebrows.'

'The boy must not be allowed to get away with it!'

'Supposing it's a girl?' teased Basher.

'Either way, I will leave no stone unturned until I've tracked the person down. He or she must be punished!'

'Oh, come on now,' said the Welshman with a grin.

'Let's not get this out of proportion. There's no malice here. If I thought there was, I'd have beaten the daylights out of him when he called round.'

'Who?'

'The anonymous artist, of course.'

'You *know* who it is?'

'Of course, mun. There's only one kid who can draw that well and who'd have the cheek to send the thing. Damien Taylor.'

'And he actually *came* here?'

'Last night. Cheered me up no end.'

'I'll speak to the boy.'

'Forget it. Apart from anything else, it's not a school matter. Took place off the premises. And I'm not complaining.'

'Well . . .'

Froggy fulminated for some while then agreed to drop the matter. Distant envy stirred in him once again. No pupil would ever show the slightest interest in paying him a visit at home.

Basher gazed wistfully up at the cartoon.

'Wish it had been Everest.'

'What?'

'Sounds better than Snowdon. Maddening thing was, I was nowhere near the top. My foot slipped when I was halfway up. I think my climbing days are over.'

'Can you get about at all?'

'Yes. Went out for a five-mile run this morning.' Basher slapped his injured leg in exasperation. 'If only I could. But I'm not supposed to put any weight on it. They gave me some crutches at the hospital but I can get around the house on a walking stick.'

'Don't overdo it, Mr Bowen.'

'I wasn't cut out for lying about and doing nothing.'

'How much longer will it be?'

'Weeks!' said the other gloomily.

Froggy brought him up to date with school news then started to take his leave. He had only called in briefly on his way to a meeting at the education office. Basher reached for his stick.

'No, no, don't get up,' insisted the other. 'I can see myself out. You get some rest.'

'I get nothing *but* rest!' moaned Basher.

The headmaster walked to the door then paused.

'One consolation, anyway.'

'What's that?'

'The Ainsley Annexe is in good hands while you're away.'

'Is it?'

'Mr Stanley has established a Reign of Terror there.'

'So I hear.'

'It must put your mind at ease.'

'Why?'

'To know that everything is under control. You don't have to fret about coming back. Mr Stanley is managing superbly.'

Froggy gave a final wave then went out.

Basher Bowen reflected on what had just been said and he became more and more annoyed. The implication was that Soldier Stan was doing his job better than he did and that hurt his pride. He also knew that it was not true. If he was given his head for too long, Soldier Stan could do a lot of damage at the Sin Bin. It was disturbing.

Basher hauled himself up and hopped on one foot to the hall. Grabbing his aluminium crutches, he fitted them under his arms and opened the front door. He was going for a walk.

* * *

111

Don Sheen's lesson that afternoon was interesting enough but Tariq was not engaged in it at all. His mind was on fire. He was feeling more isolated than ever. Woodfield was a constant source of misery and there was no relief from it at home. His father was coming down hard on him and even Soraya was now urging him to forget Natasha. It was galling. He would show them all.

By the time the lesson came to an end, he had reached a vital decision. He would act on it immediately. Most of the kids raced out of the Sin Bin as soon as they could but he hung back to speak to a friend.

'Cal . . .'

'Yeah?'

'Can I ask you a favour?'

'You can *arsk* it. I'm nor promisin' to do it.'

'Will you deliver a message for me?'

'Who to?'

'Mr Stanley.'

'Nor me, mate. Bite my bleedin' 'ead orff.'

'Please, Cal. Means a lot to me.'

'Why?'

'Just do it, will you?'

Calvin Hubberd could see the pleading look in the other's eyes. This was no casual request. Tariq was in trouble and needed a helping hand. The Jamaican boy nodded.

'If iss thar important, mate . . .'

'It is.'

'OK, then.'

'Thanks, Cal. There's something else as well.'

'What?'

'Find Soraya. Tell her to go back on her own.'

'Shall I say where you are?'

'No.'

'She's bound to ask.'

'That's her problem.'

Calvin was shocked. Tariq was usually so considerate and protective where his sister was concerned. What had happened to make him brush her aside like that?

Tariq scribbled a note, folded the paper and handed it over.

'You know nothing, remember.'

'Nothin' at all, mate.'

'You've no idea where I am.'

'None.'

'And I didn't say anything to you as I left.'

'Norra dicky bird.'

'Good. You'd better be on your way.'

They left the Annexe and came out into the street. The first wave of kids was rolling through the gates of the main school. The sight of the massed uniforms served to confirm Tariq in his decision. Woodfield was enemy territory. He did not belong.

'See you, Cal,' he mumbled.

'Good luck!'

'Thanks.'

'Enjoy the trip.'

Tariq was startled. The gap-toothed grin and the twinkle in Calvin's eyes showed that he had guessed. More important, he would keep the secret. Tariq squeezed his shoulder in thanks then ran off in the direction of the bus station.

Fifteen minutes later, he was dropped off a couple of miles outside the city. He walked the short distance to the access road. Above his head, traffic thundered along the M6. As vehicles approached the access road to join the motorway, the boy jabbed his thumb in the air in the hope of hitching a lift. But nobody stopped. Almost an hour passed and every vehicle ignored him. His plan was being frustrated at the very outset.

Just as he was losing heart, a lorry slowed down and came to a grinding halt. The passenger door opened and the driver invited him to get in. Tariq climbed up into the cab and found himself sitting next to a burly young man in overalls.

'Where you going to, mate?' asked the driver.

'Glasgow.'

Chapter Ten

Calvin Hubberd would not have missed it for the world. It was a moment to savour. He never thought that he would actually enjoy being with Soldier Stan but he was mistaken. In the presence of the teacher, he usually felt profoundly uncomfortable. This time, the boot was on the other foot.

Soldier Stan was waiting in the entrance hall at the main school, festering with impatience. Evidently, he was in his most irascible mood and needed to be approached with care.

Calvin sidled up to him and coughed quietly.

'What do you want, Hubberd?'

'I've gorra message for you, sir.'

'From whom?'

'Tariq.'

'Have you!' growled the teacher.

Calvin handed over the piece of paper and Soldier Stan unfolded it to read the message. His manner altered at once. Fury became astonishment. His eyes widened, his mouth opened and he let out a wheeze of sheer surprise. Calvin glowed. He would have paid to see this. Soldier Stan with the wind taken out of him.

The teacher fought to recover his equanimity.

'Er, when did he give you this?'

'Juss now, sir.'

'Did he say where he was going?'

'No, sir.'

'Or why he was not coming to see me?'

'Norra word, sir.'

'Are you *sure*, Hubberd.'

'Doan know nothin', sir. Honess!'

Soldier Stan read the note again and his jaw tightened. Calvin could not resist a parting quip.

'Will there be any reply, sir?'

'Get out!'

'Yes, sir.'

'Vanish, you imbecile!'

The Jamaican boy ran out through the door at speed. He had seen the feared Soldier Stan routed. It was priceless. He burst into peals of laughter and skipped off across the yard.

Harry Stanley, meanwhile, stood there and glowered. He risked a third glance at the note before scrunching it up and stuffing it into his pocket.

He stalked off down the corridor with eyes ablaze.

When Soraya came home alone again, her father knew that something was wrong. He cross-examined her at once.

'He must have said something.'

'He didn't, Father.'

'What about this boy who spoke to you?'

'Calvin Hubberd?'

'Did he have any idea where Tariq was going?'

'No. He just passed on the message.'

Atlas Jahan walked up and down the living room like a caged tiger. Since his son had started at Woodfield, he had been nothing but trouble. It was time that he was sorted out properly. Mo would never have done anything like this. He was an obedient and hard-working youth who always put the family first. Tariq had a mind of his own. It was a dangerous quality.

Something else preyed on his father's mind. He was convinced that his younger son knew who was responsible

for the acts of vandalism at the Ace Garage yet Tariq
would reveal no names. It was infuriating. Atlas had twice
come close to trying to beat the information out of the
boy.

Soraya watched him nervously and defended her
brother.

'Tariq is a good boy at heart.'

'I wish he was!' said her father ruefully.

'There's some very simple explanation for this.'

'He wants to get back at me.'

'No.'

'Then why is he disobeying me?'

'Maybe he had no choice.'

'What?'

'They might have kept him in after school or something.'

'This other boy would have mentioned that.'

'Not if he didn't want us to know about it,' argued
Soraya. 'He was probably afraid of what you'd say.'

'I'll say plenty!' vowed Atlas.

'Don't be too hard on him. Tariq is – '

'I'll deal with him my way.'

'He doesn't mean to be – '

'That's enough, Soraya,' interrupted her father, bringing
the conversation to an end. 'You can get on with your
homework. I have to make a phone call.'

Soraya nodded and went off meekly to her room. She
was deeply alarmed on her brother's behalf and she regretted talking to him about Natasha the way that she had. It
had clearly upset him. At this stage, even Soraya did not
realize quite how much.

Her words to Tariq had been the last straw.

Harry Stanley was a man with the courage to admit when
he had made a mistake. He came into the staff room, saw

117

Don Sheen lounging in a chair and went straight over to him. Taking a five pound note from his wallet, he offered it to his colleague.

'What's this for, Harry?'

'I'm honouring my bet.'

'Eh?'

'I put Jahan in detention today. He didn't turn up.'

'Oh, I see.'

'I was wrong about him.'

He thrust the money into Don's hand and went out. Don Sheen felt at once pleased and worried. It was heartening to get the better of Soldier Stan like that but there might be severe repercussions for the boy. The first time he cut detention, Tariq was sentenced to a term at the Sin Bin. A far worse punishment might follow this second outrage.

The staff room telephone rang but he paid no heed. He put the five pound note in his wallet and pondered anew. He recalled that Tariq had been very preoccupied during the lesson that afternoon. What was on the boy's mind?

Anthea Craig had answered the telephone.

'Don!' she called.

'Yeah?'

'I think you'd better take this, please.'

'Who is it?'

'Mr Jahan.'

'Be right there.'

He leaped up and hurried over to the wall. Mrs Craig gave him the receiver and lifted her eyebrows inquisitively. Then she went over to get herself a cup of tea from the urn.

'Hello,' said Don. 'Mr Jahan.'

'That is Mr Sheen?'

'Yes. What's the problem?'

118

'Tariq has not come home.'

'Oh.'

'I wondered if he was still at school.'

'Er, no, I'm afraid he's not, Mr Jahan,' said the teacher. 'But he was supposed to. Mr Stanley put him on detention.'

'And he did not turn up!' The father sounded mortified. 'This is terrible, Mr Sheen. The second time!'

'I can't imagine Tariq would do such a thing without a very good reason. Any idea where he is?'

'None. That's why I rang you. All Soraya was told was that she was to come home alone.'

Don did his best to soothe the father but it was not easy. Atlas was greatly troubled. He veered between anxiety and rage, worried that something might happen to his son yet vowing to punish him severely when he came back.

'Listen,' said Don. 'I have to go now because I have an evening class but I'll check back in later, if I may. Could you give me the number, please?

'Of course.'

When Don had jutted down the number of the Ace Garage, he rung off. All pleasure at winning the fiver off Soldier Stan had evaporated. He was filled with concern for Tariq. The boy was single-minded and impulsive. Don hoped that he had not been provoked into doing something ill-considered and dramatic. As he strolled towards his evening class, one question assailed him.

Where *was* Tariq?

It was much more difficult than he had imagined. The lorry could only take him as far as the Sandbach services on the M6. There was a long delay as he tried to thumb another lift. Eventually, a transit van took him on up to Penrith. The wait was even longer this time. Most vehicles shot past without giving him a second glance. One or two of the drivers who did see him made abusive gestures. Time was rolling on. It was dark.

A milk lorry came to his rescue. It reeked of its cargo and lumbered along but it was at least a lift. Tariq had to put up with the rambling monologue of the old man at the wheel but it was a small price to pay. At long last – not far short of midnight – he was dropped off near his old home.

The garage was empty and boarded up. Tariq's stomach lurched. He had lived in the premises at the back of the garage all his life. To see it in such a sorry and neglected state was a shock to him. It was symbolic.

Breaking into a run, he dashed through the streets that he knew so well, twisting and turning until he came to the road where Natasha lived. There was a light on. His heart lifted. He had envisaged the reunion so often in his mind that it had hardened into fact. Natasha would see him, burst into tears of joy then fling herself into his arms. Nothing else would matter.

Cold reality now hit him. Supposing her parents answered the door? Supposing they would not even let him see Natasha? If she was still ill, she might be in bed asleep. What was he to do then? As he stood in front of her house, he realized that he had no contingency plans at all. Everything hinged on Natasha's response and he had taken it for granted.

Doubts held back his hand when he raised it to knock the door. Would it be better to wait until morning? If so, where could he spend the night? It had to be now. The impetus which had carried him all the way north from the Midlands took him that final step. Summoning up his courage, he knocked on the door. There was no reply. He knocked louder. The door to the hall opened and a light

120

was switched on. Through the bubble-glass of the front door, he could see a figure moving hazily towards him.

'Who is it?' asked an anxious female voice.

It was Natasha. His dream had been fulfilled.

'It's me, Natasha. It's Tariq.'

'Who?'

'Tariq. Tariq Jahan.'

'Never!'

She unlocked the door and opened it wide. Expecting to see her in the blue dress that had fired his imagination for so long, he was disappointed to find her in a quilted dressing gown and fluffy slippers. For her part, the girl was astounded.

'What on earth are you doing here?'

'I came to see you.'

'What?'

'I ran away. To be with you.'

'*Why*?'

One word rocked him completely. Instead of welcoming him with open arms, Natasha was plainly confused. Even embarrassed. Something had happened since they had last met. The magic had disappeared. The bond between them – on her side – had weakened.

'Can I come in?' he whispered.

'Well . . .'

'Please, Natasha. I've come all this way.'

'OK. But only for a wee while.'

She took him into the lounge and offered him a seat. As he lowered himself on the sofa, she made a point of sitting on an upright chair opposite him. It was another blow to his high expectations. His confidence began to seep away.

Natasha had changed. She still had the quiet beauty that had attracted him in the first place but it was tarnished by a severe frown. There was an underlying hardness to her manner. He groped for something to say to her.

'Where are your parents?'

'Away at my uncle's house. I've been looking after my sister. She's in bed. I was just about to go up myself.' She shook her head in disbelief. 'You really ran away to come here?'

'My father wouldn't let me come otherwise.'

'Maybe he was right,' she said levelly.

He was rocked again. Where was his beloved?

'Zaitoon wrote to Soraya that you were ill.'

'Well . . . aye . . .'

'And she said that your father stopped you reading my letters. Is that right, Natasha?'

'Yes,' she said, without conviction.

'So my get-well card never reached you?'

'No, Tariq. I'm sorry . . .'

He had never felt so ill at ease before. Sustained by a vision of Natasha and of a future together with her, he had risked everything and made his way back. But she had not expected him and was not overjoyed to see him. As she lowered her head and bit her lip, he saw that she was in great discomfort as well.

He tried to rally her with his warmest memory.

'D'you ever think about that outing to the Highlands?'

'Now and again.'

'I do, Natasha. I'll never forget what you said to me.'

'It was a long time ago, Tariq.'

'No matter.'

She gave him a wistful smile. It restored some of his confidence. He stood up and took a step towards her. Natasha tensed in alarm. He saw her fists clench.

'I miss you,' he said. 'I want to be with you.'

'That's no possible, Tariq,' she whispered.

'Why not?'

'I'm to be married next month.'

The breath was taken right out of him. Married! The girl had more or less promised him that she would be *his* wife. He had built his plans around her. What had gone wrong?

Natasha shrugged helplessly and gabbled an explanation.

'It was nice when you were here, Tariq. It was special to me. But it was different when you went away. I saw all the things that were against us. There were just too many of them. Then my father flew to Karachi a couple of weeks ago. When he came back, he said that a marriage had been arranged. We'll be going over there next month.'

'Next *month*!'

Tariq could not compete with that. It would be years before he was in any position to marry her and there would be a running battle with both families along the way. Natasha had bowed to tradition. She was submitting to her parents' wishes.

The truth oozed slowly out. She was not ill and her father had not intercepted Tariq's letters. They were both excuses to explain why she had not written herself. In time, she hoped, he would lose interest. She was trying to let him down lightly.

Tariq was shattered. The situation was just too big for him to handle. A dream which had kept him going for months had now turned into a nightmare.

'You'll no be able to stay here.'

'What?'

'Can you go to your Uncle Roshan's?'

He had no idea what to do except that he had to get out. Natasha had hurt him enough for one night. He stumbled to the door, opened it wide and went out into the night. The crisp air hit him like a slap across the face. Turning into the road, he surged blindly on. When he was heading for Glasgow, he had a purpose and a destination. Both had been cruelly wrested from him. He had been cut adrift.

Pancho Reeves and Mike O'Brien waited until Graham had finished tidying everything away. They had called at the pub earlier and had no difficulty in being served. In jeans and bomber jackets, they looked over eighteen. They had several glasses of beer and Graham managed to sink a pint or two himself. It was now time to go.

Pancho deferred to his brother as leader.

'Wor we gonna do to it, Gray?'

''it the place like a bleedin' 'urricane!'

'Less smash the winders!' suggested Mike.

'Thass the least we'll do!' promised Graham. 'Refusin' to serve me petrol. I'll teach them Pakis.'

They walked through the precinct then took a short cut across the car park. It was a familiar hunting ground for Graham and his instinct alerted him.

'Quick! Down there!'

They ducked behind a parked van as ordered.

'Wass up?' asked Pancho.

'You always wanted to come on a job, didden you?'

'Yeah, Gray.'

'Now's your chance, our kid.'

They peered round the van. A solitary figure was coming towards them across the deserted car park. He was a well-dressed Pakistani in his twenties. Graham sniffed money. He outlined the plan of attack in a hoarse whisper.

'When I say, juss get be'ind 'im. OK?'

'Right.'

'Leave it to us.'

'I'll do the talkin'. If he gives us what we want, I'll lerrim off with a couple of thumps. If he tries to run, we all belt him. Gorrit?'

The others nodded. Robbing a hapless Pakistani was an incidental bonus. It would put them in exactly the right mood to wreak havoc at the Ace Garage.

The man got closer and closer. Graham waited.

'Now!' he snarled.

He jumped out to confront the pedestrian. His accomplices stood behind the victim and gave him a few shoves. The Pakistani smiled and hunched his shoulders.

'What do you want of me?'

'Money!' grunted Graham. 'Give us your wallet.'

'But why?'

''cos we'll kick 'ell out of you if you don't.'

'Please, no . . .'

The Pakistani opened his coat to reach inside but he did not produce a wallet. A truncheon suddenly appeared in his hand and he swept it in a circle to drive them away. Before they could move in on him again, they were aware of figures running towards them. Six young men cornered them and pinioned them.

'Police!' announced one. 'You're nicked.'

The Pakistani strode over to them with a smile.

'Detective-Constable Patel,' he introduced. 'We've been after you for a long time. You're finished.'

Protesting loudly, the three of them were dragged away.

The police trap worked superbly. Three youths were now in custody and the Ace Garage had been saved from attack. Graham, Pancho and Mike would not be Paki-bashing for some time.

The police ended Tariq's midnight stroll as well. When they found him meandering around Glasgow city centre, they asked him who he was and where he was going. When he told them about his Uncle Roshan, they drove him around there at once. Roshan was older, bigger and more effusive than his brother, Atlas. Hauled out of his bed by the police, he did not mind at all when he saw that they had his nephew. He welcomed the boy in and his wife made tea at once. Having gleaned enough of the story, he rang Atlas.

His brother was in tears at the other end of the line. When Tariq went on to speak to him, his father was not angry at all. He was overwhelmed with relief. He explained that Don Sheen had called in on his way back from the evening class and was, in fact, still there. Don had made him understand the pressures that his son was under.

'Will you come home to us, Tariq?'

'Yes.'

'Catch a train tomorrow. Uncle Roshan will lend you the money.'

When he put the receiver down, there was a lump in the boy's throat. Natasha had spurned him but his family were still there. Perhaps it was as well to make a complete break with Scotland.

He would give the new life a proper chance.

Monday morning brought its usual round of moans from the kids who converged on Woodfield School but none of them approached the place with as much apprehension as Tariq Jahan. It was his first day back since defying Soldier Stan's order. He could imagine the roasting he would have to face. When he fled from the place, he did not stop to consider the consequences. They weighed on him now.

He gulped when he saw the Annexe. Soraya put a comforting hand on his shoulder. He gave her a thin smile.

'Don't be afraid, Tariq.'

'It'll no be very nice,' he sighed.

'Go in and get it over with.'

He nodded. Straightening up, he crossed the road and

went up the steps and in through the door. He expected Soldier Stan to be waiting for him in the corridor but there was no sign of him so he went straight on in to the classroom.

'Who the hell are you?'

A big, brawny man with thick eyebrows was seated at the desk. Aluminium crutches leaned against the wall behind him.

'Tariq Jahan, sir.'

Basher laughed. 'A Scotch Pakistani! Now I've heard everything. Mind you, some of your compatriots speak with a Welsh accent where I come from. Daresay you'd find *that* funny.'

Tariq looked around nervously. The teacher grinned.

'Soldier Stan is not here, boyo. *I've* come back.'

'Are you Mr Bowen, sir?'

'That's me. Basher by name and Basher by nature. What's all this about you ignoring Mr Stanley's detention?'

'Well, yes . . . I . . .'

'Explain it later to Mr Parsons.'

'Yes, sir.'

'Today, you'll report to *me* at four o'clock.'

'If you say so, sir.'

'I do say so!' bellowed the teacher.

Tariq quailed. Basher sounded as if he could be just as unpleasant and vindictive as Soldier Stan. The Welshman then threw out a casual remark.

'And make sure you bring your squash kit.'

'Squash kit?'

'I'm giving you permission to go home at lunch time for it.'

'But why, sir?'

'Because I believe that a sporting talent should be developed, Tariq. Soldier Stan might have you picking up paper clips but I'll make you run round that court till your legs drop off. *That's* where you're going at four o'clock. To play squash.'

'Yes, sir!' said the boy with delight.

'If you're as good as Mr Sheen says you are, it'll be worth it to me. See you at four.'

'Thank you, sir!'

'And wipe that bloody big grin off your face. Hasn't anyone told you? This is the Sin Bin!'

It was business as usual. Basher was back and Tariq was rescued.